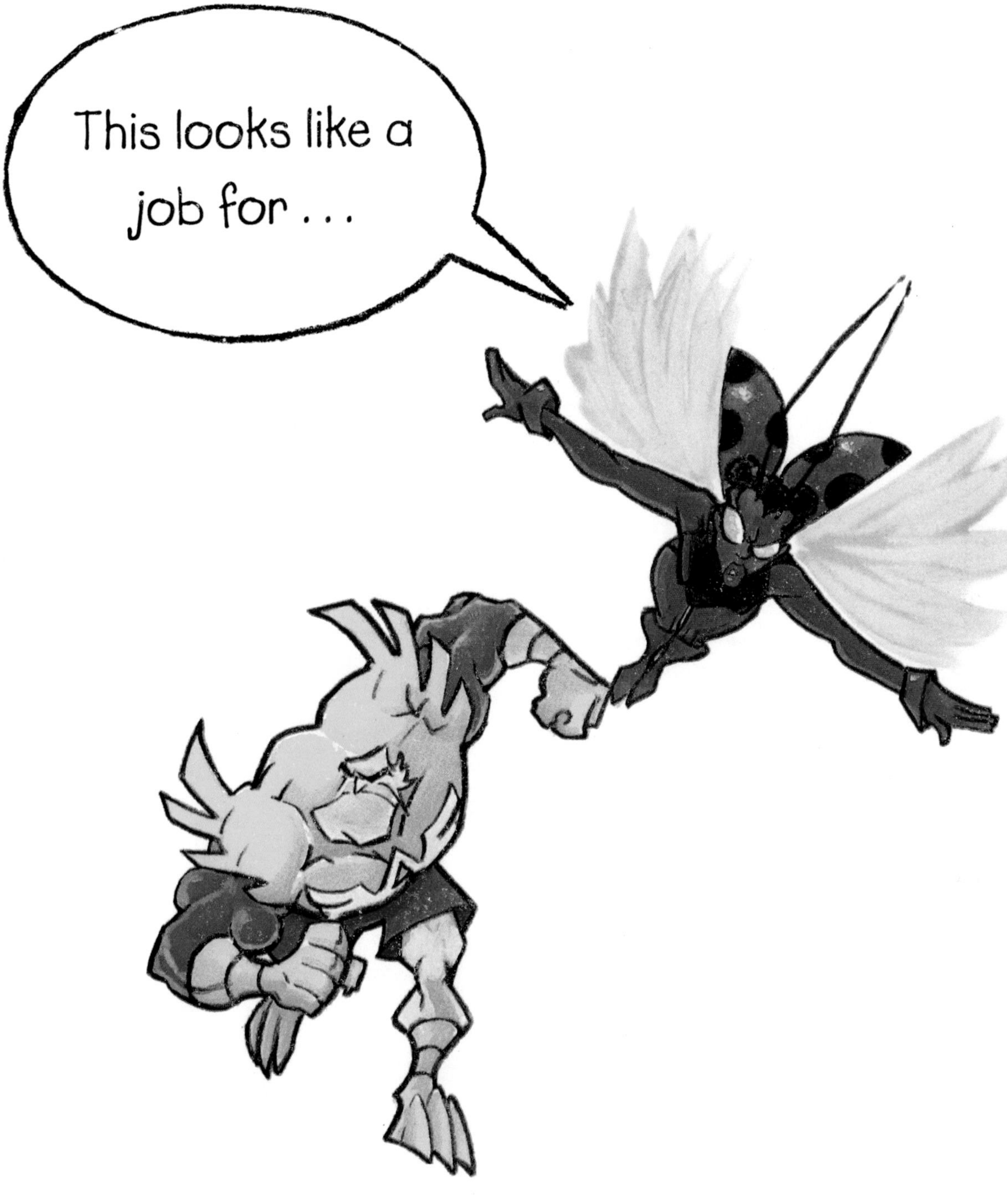
This looks like a job for . . .

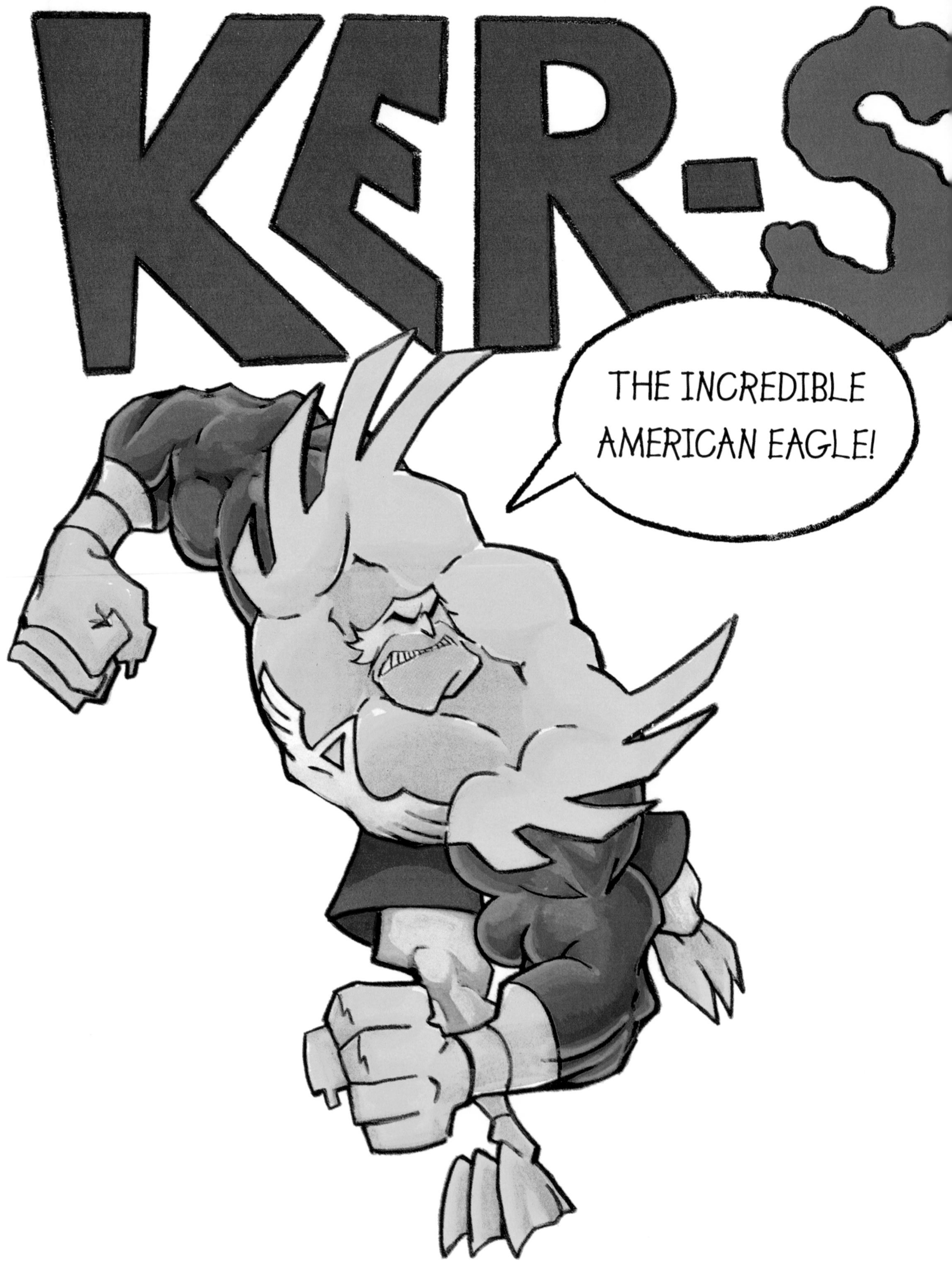
KER-S
THE INCREDIBLE AMERICAN EAGLE!

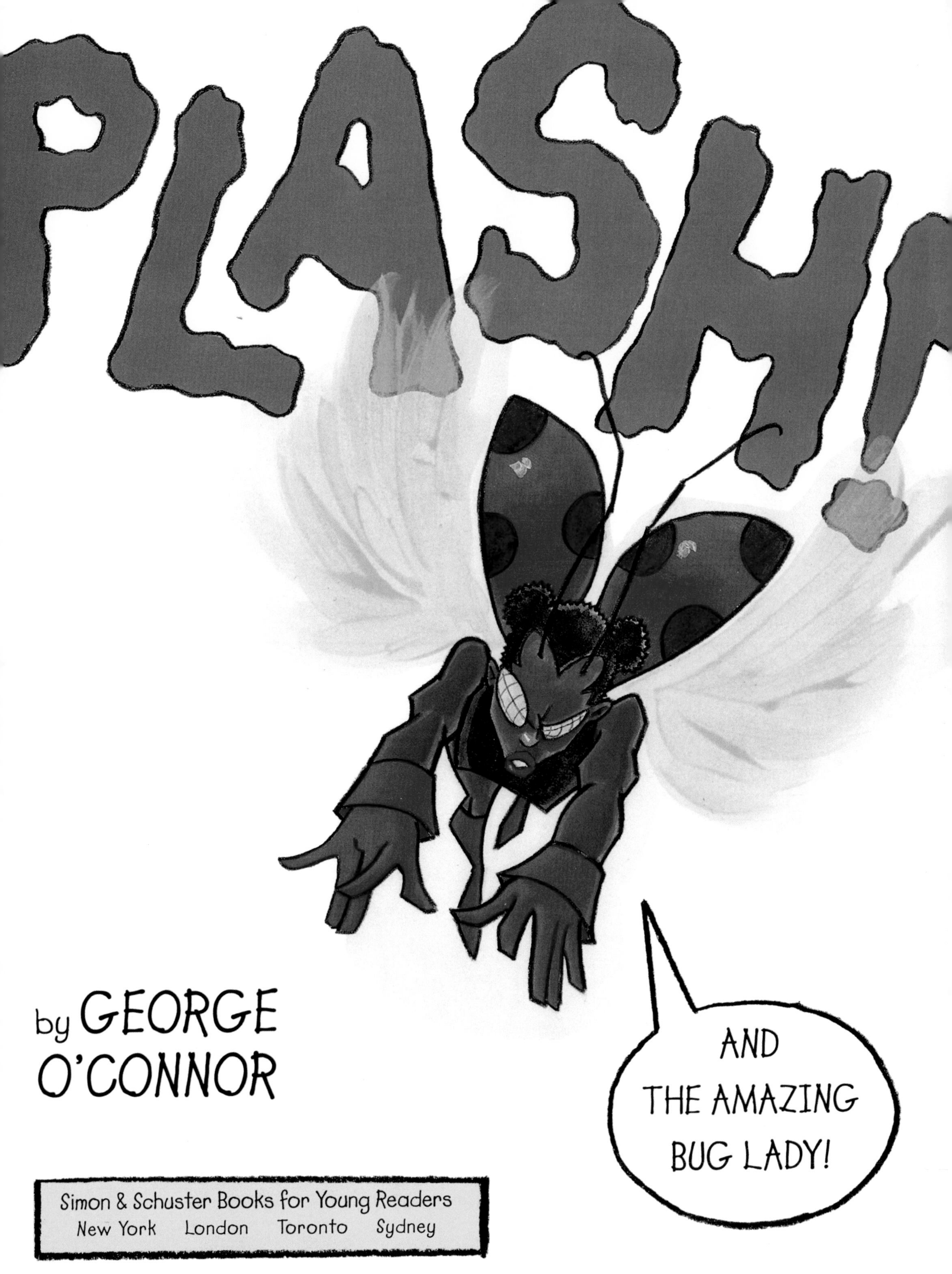
PLASH!
AND THE AMAZING BUG LADY!

by GEORGE O'CONNOR

Simon & Schuster Books for Young Readers
New York London Toronto Sydney

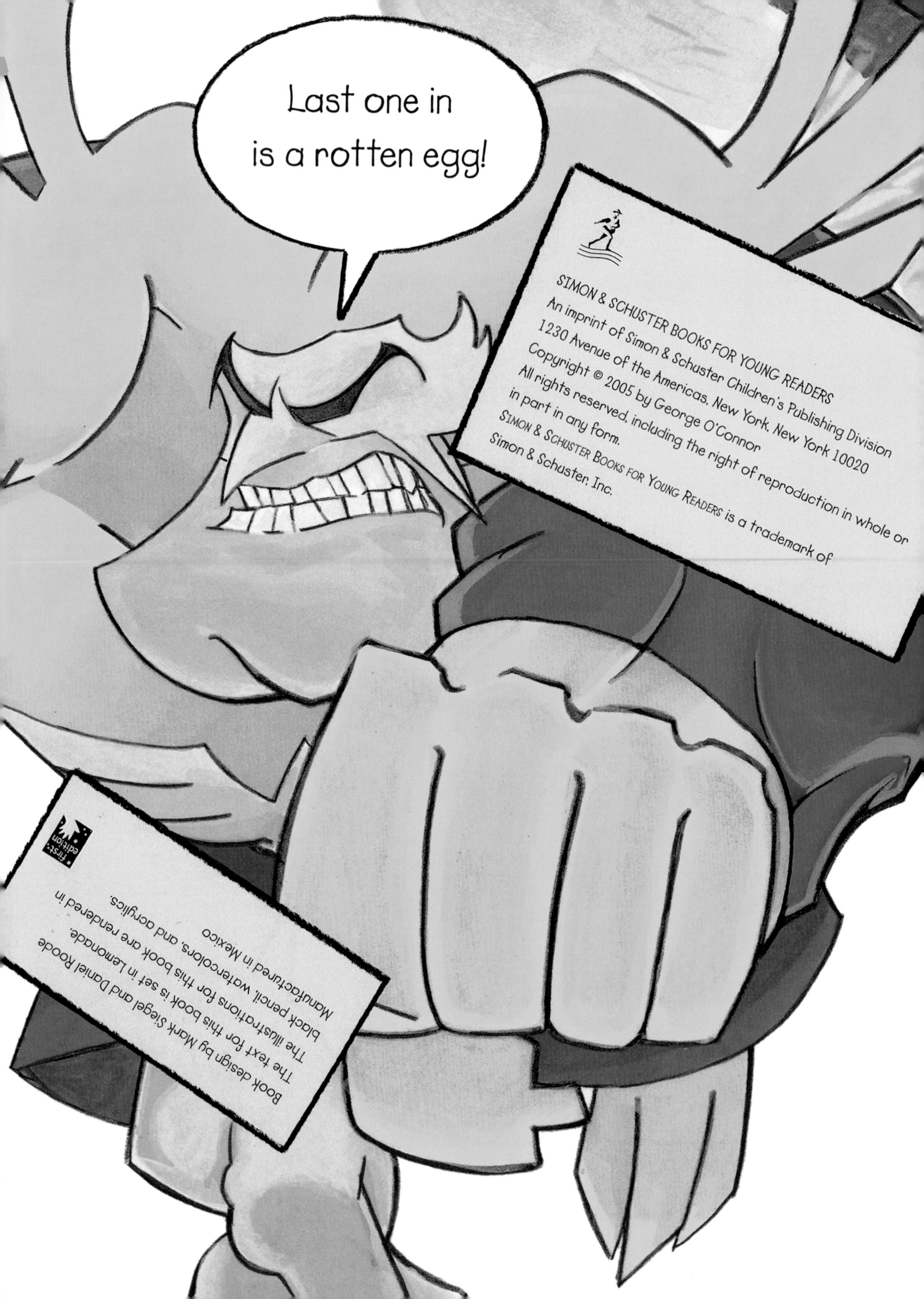
Last one in
is a rotten egg!

SIMON & SCHUSTER BOOKS FOR YOUNG READERS
An imprint of Simon & Schuster Children's Publishing Division
1230 Avenue of the Americas, New York, New York 10020

first edition
Book design by Mark Siegel and Daniel Roode
The text for this book is set in Lemonade.
The illustrations for this book are rendered in black pencil, watercolors, and acrylics.
Manufactured in Mexico

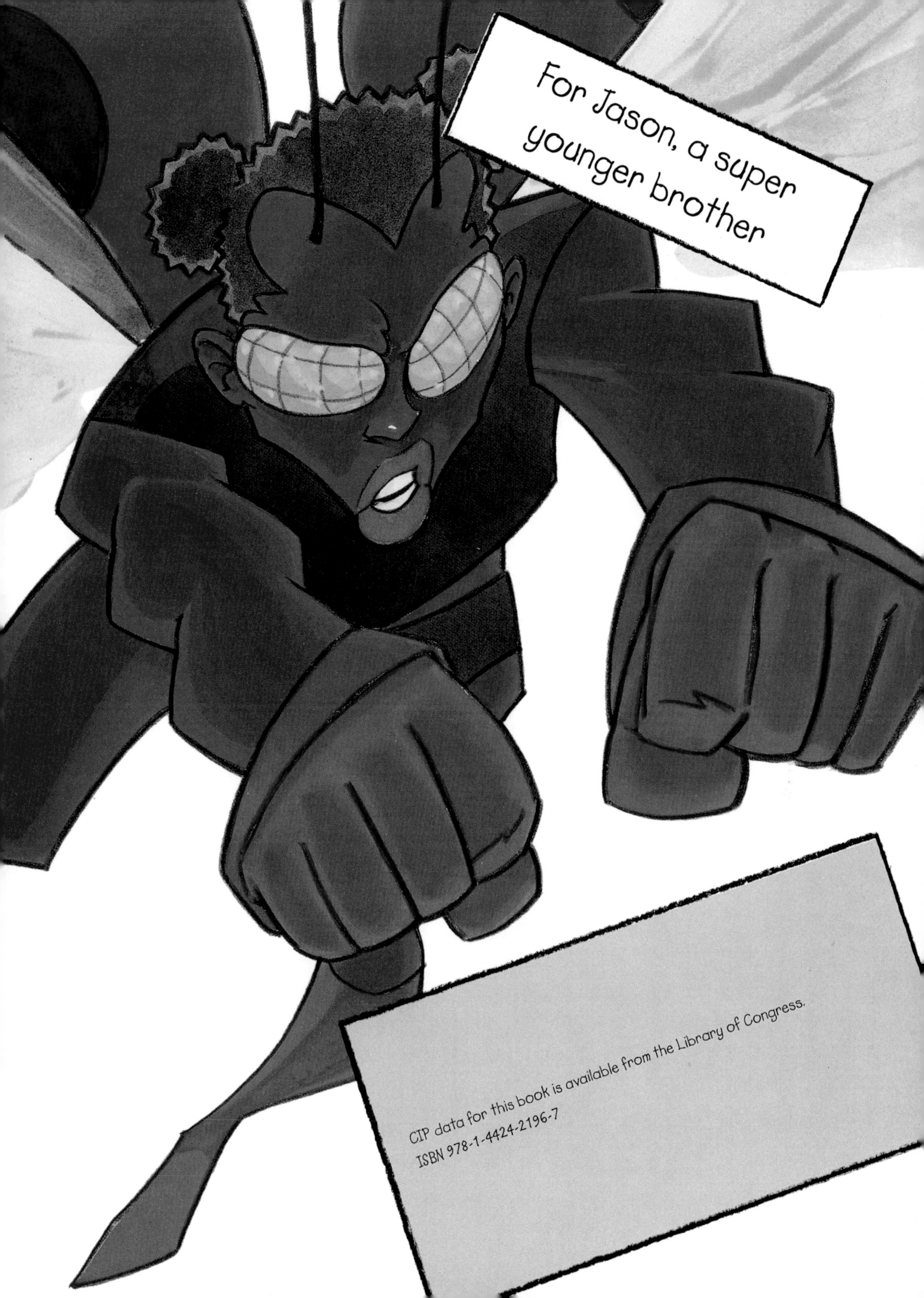

For Jason, a super younger brother

CIP data for this book is available from the Library of Congress.
ISBN 978-1-4424-2196-7

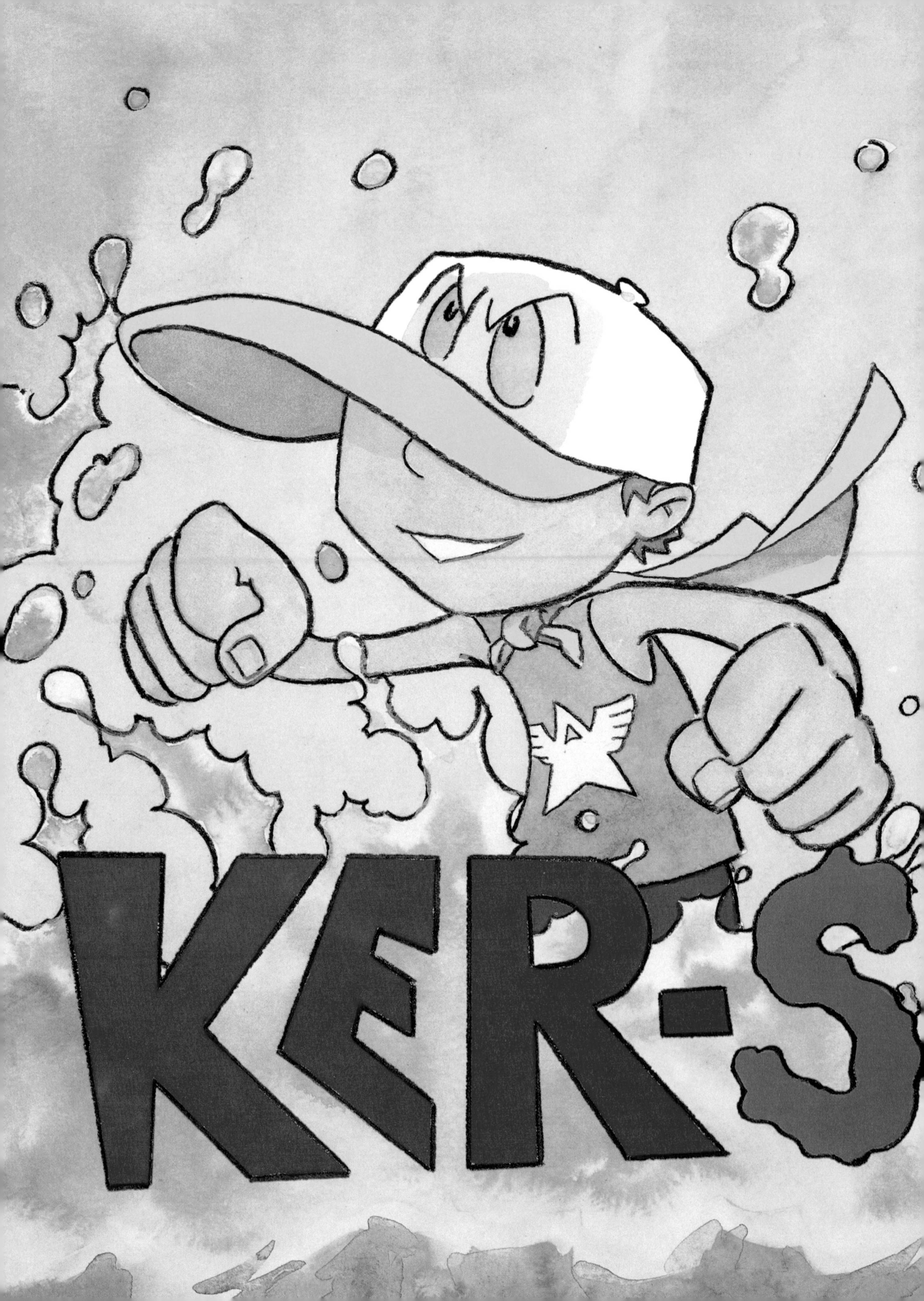
KER-S

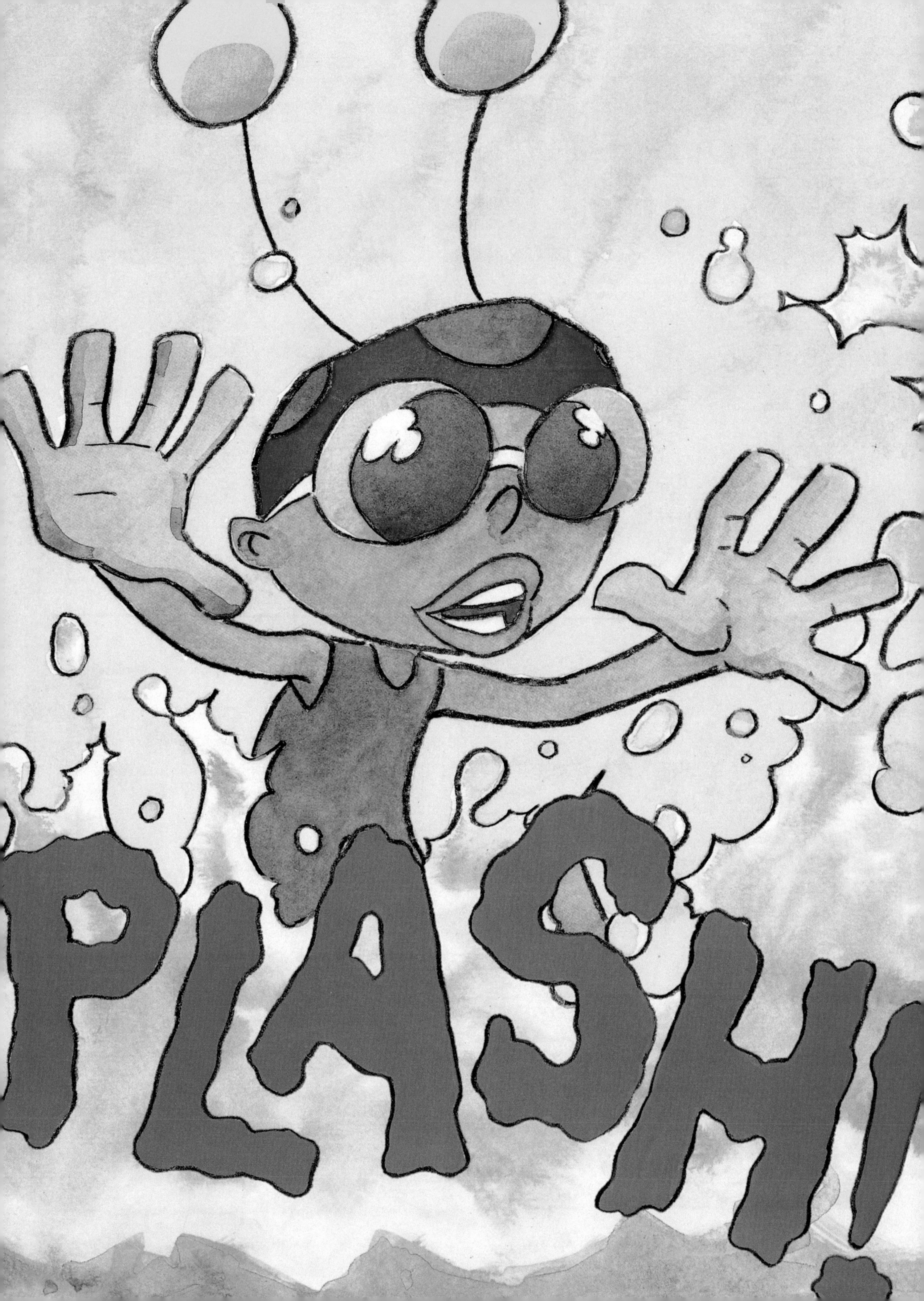
PLASH!

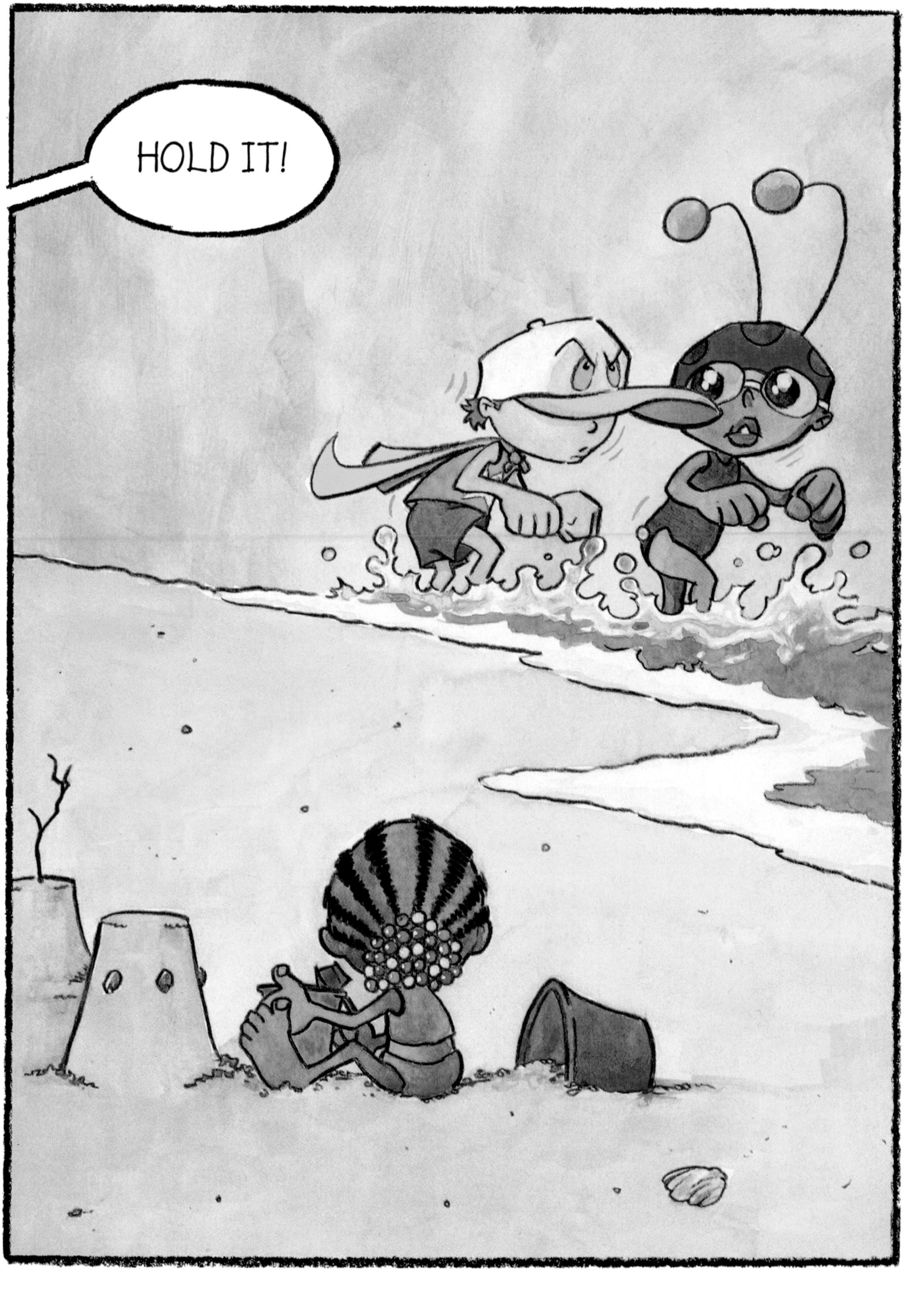
HOLD IT!

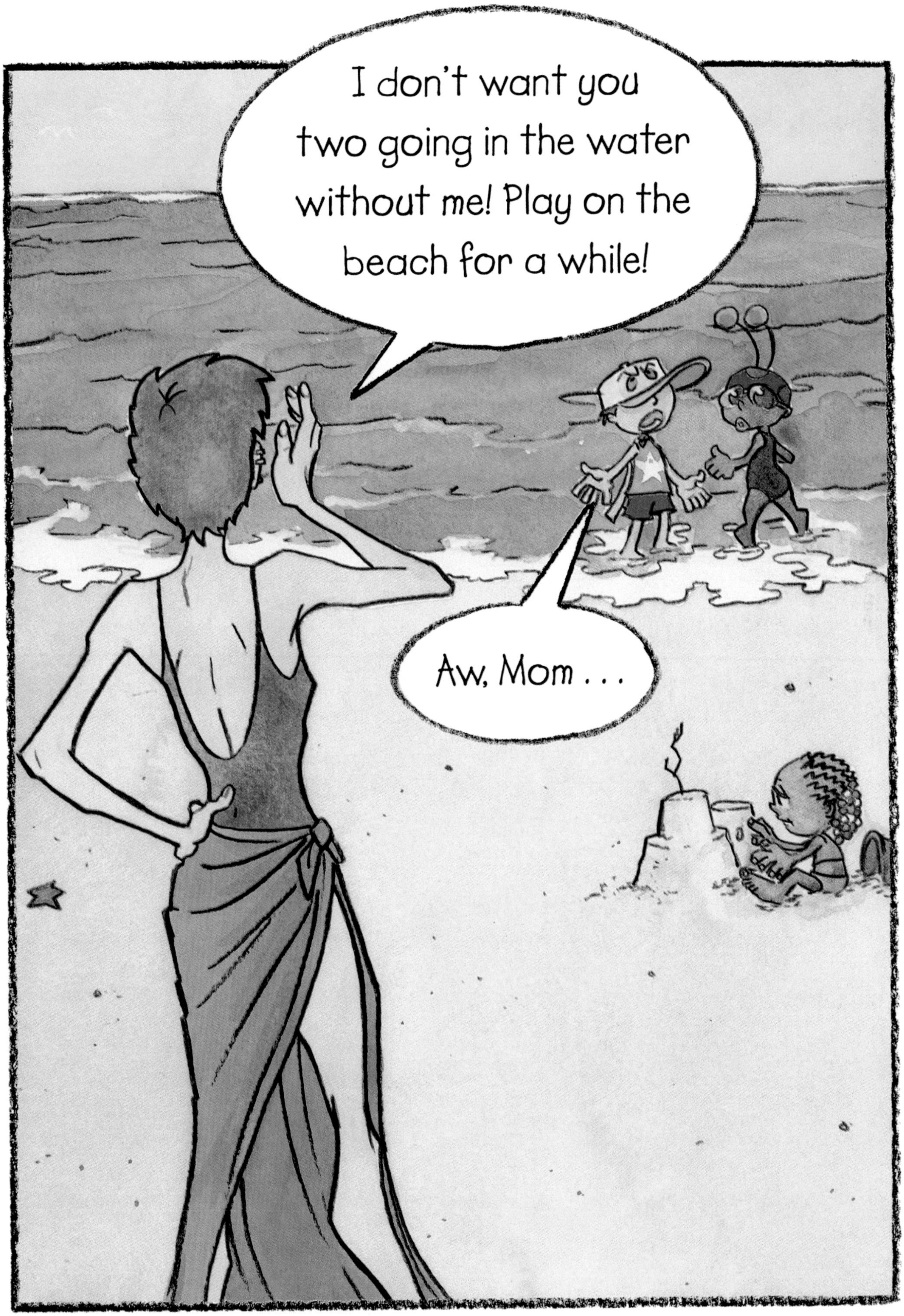
I don't want you two going in the water without *me*! Play on the beach for a while!
Aw, Mom . . .

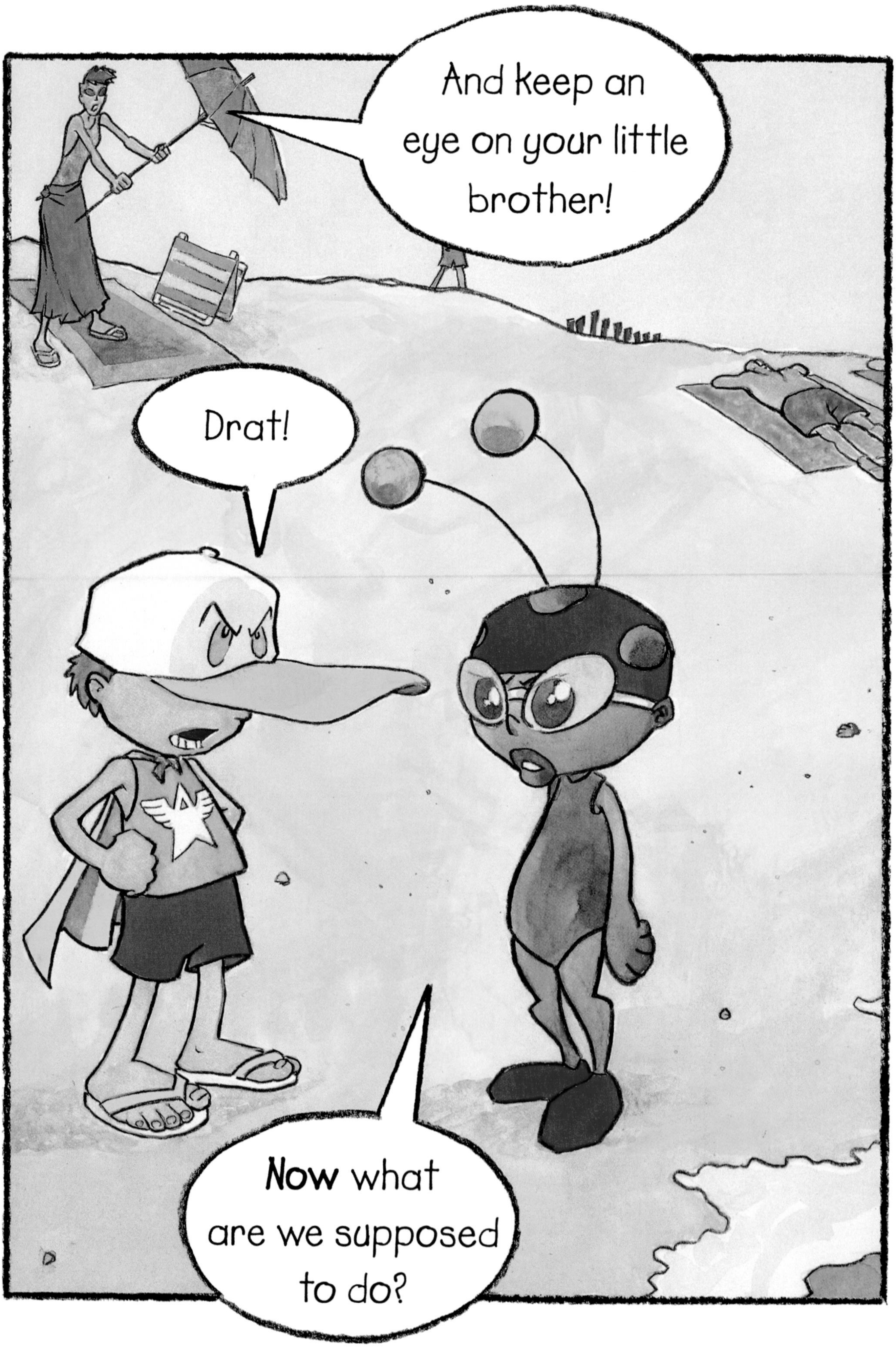
And keep an eye on your little brother!
Drat!
Now what are we supposed to do?

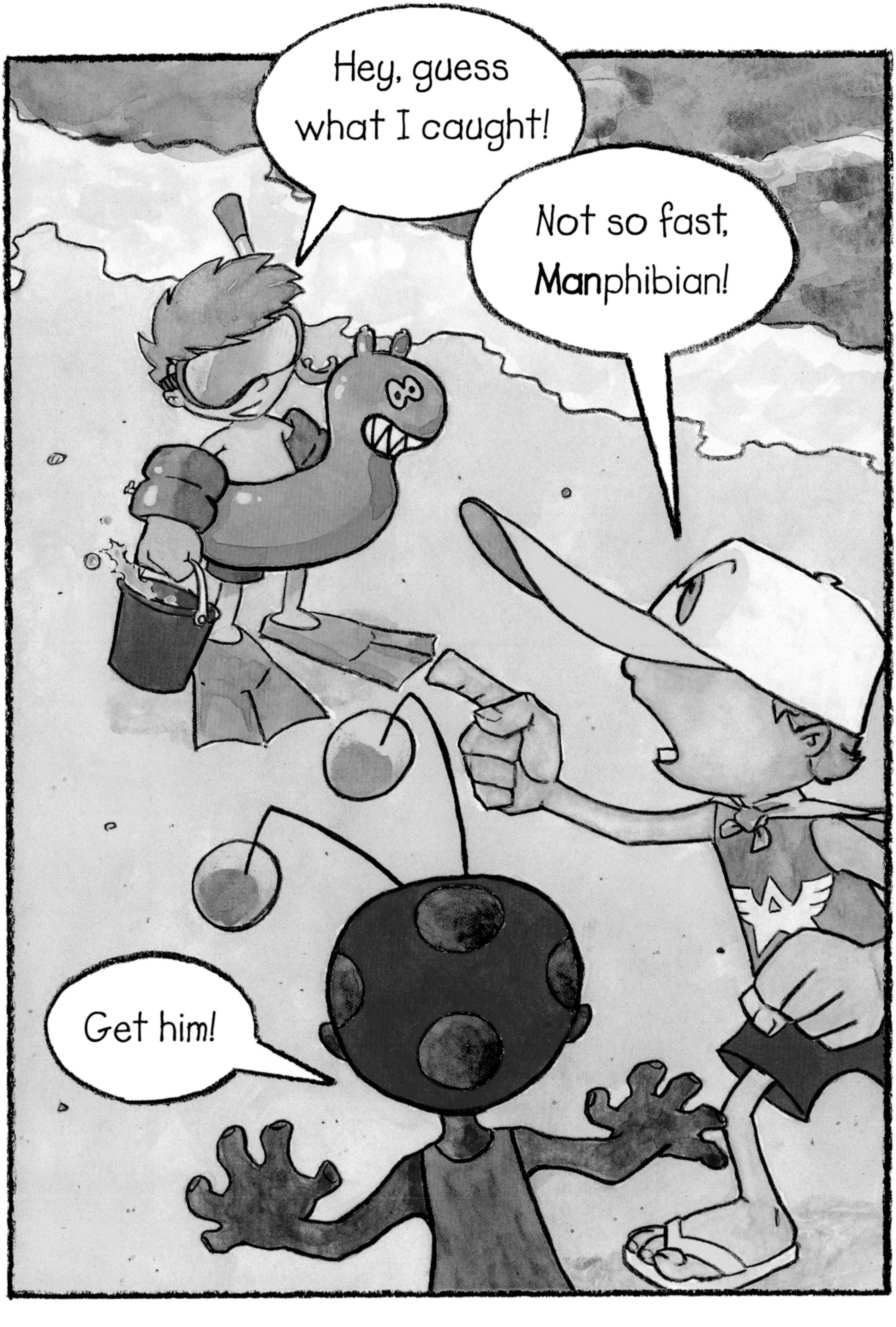
Hey, guess what I caught!
Not so fast, **Man**phibian!
Get him!

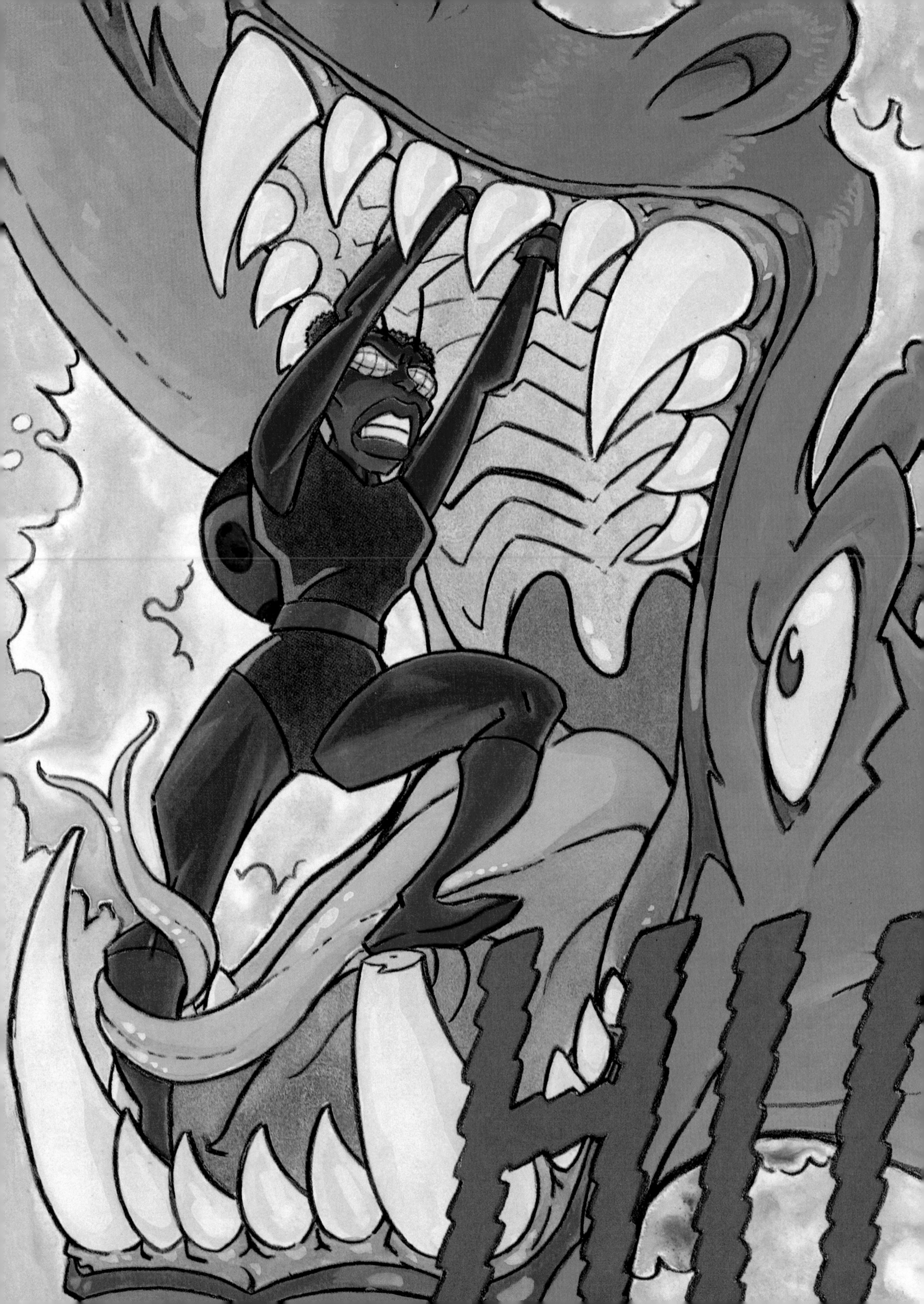

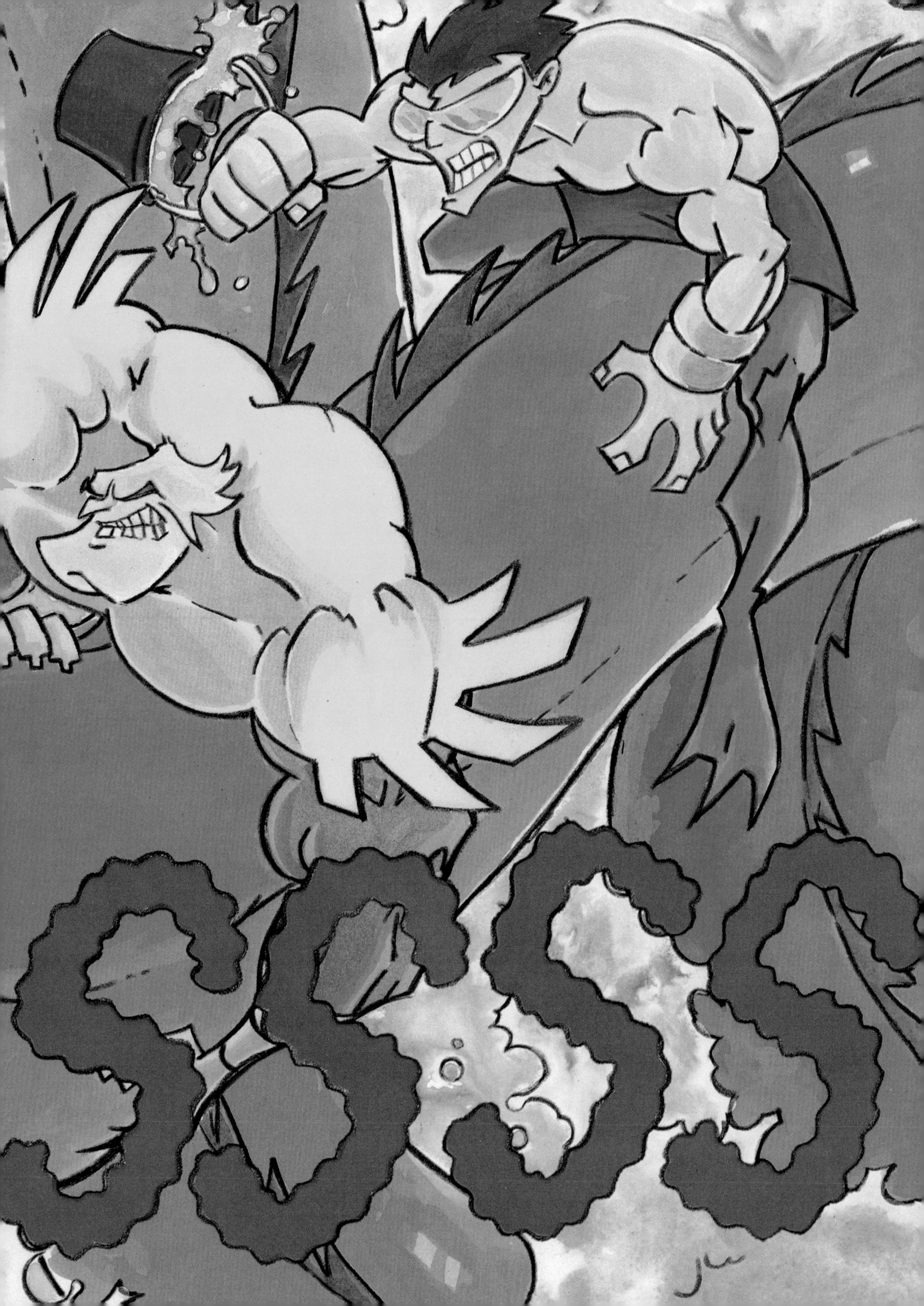
SSSS

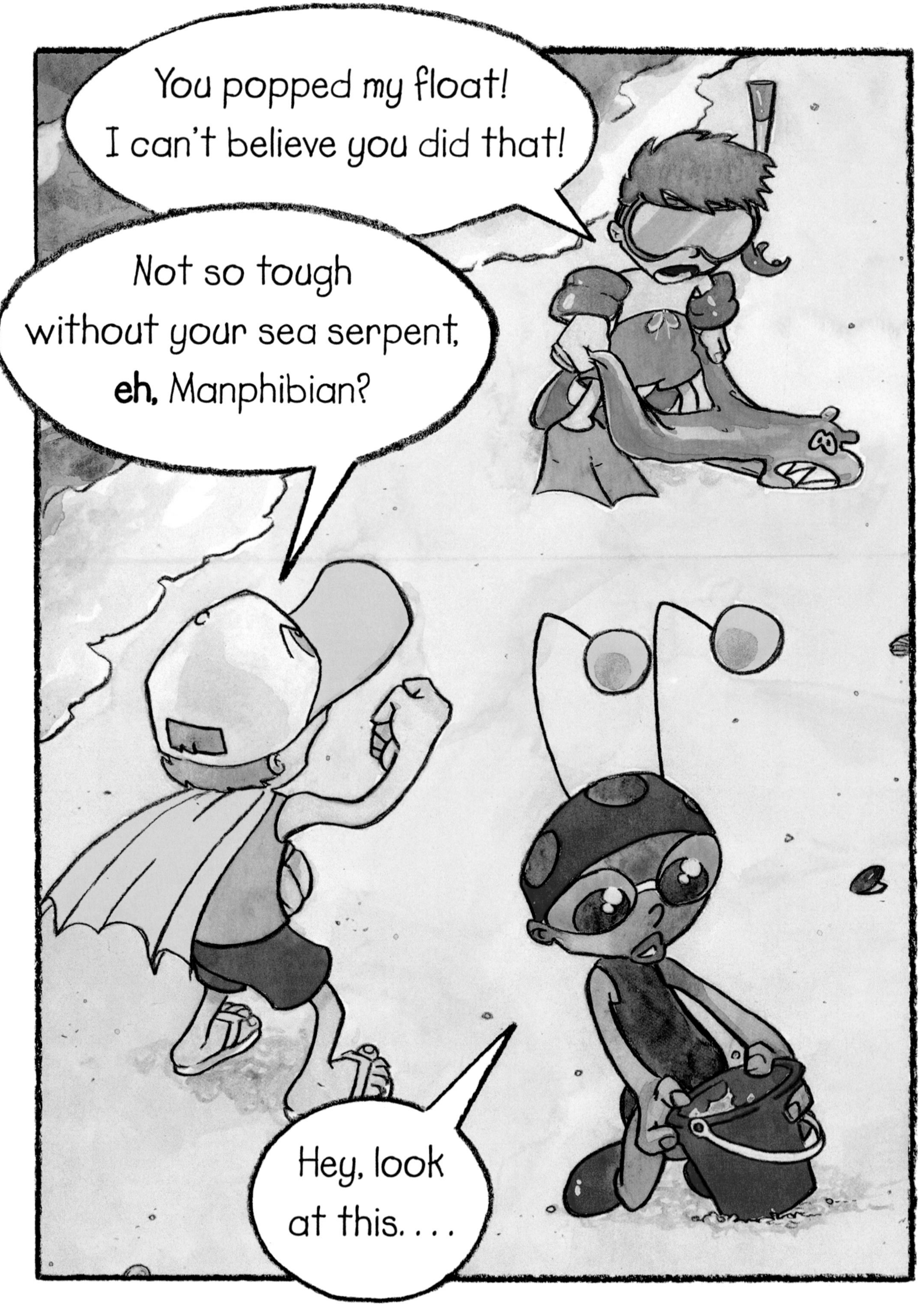
You popped my float! I can't believe you did that!
Not so tough without your sea serpent, **eh,** Manphibian?
Hey, look at this. . . .

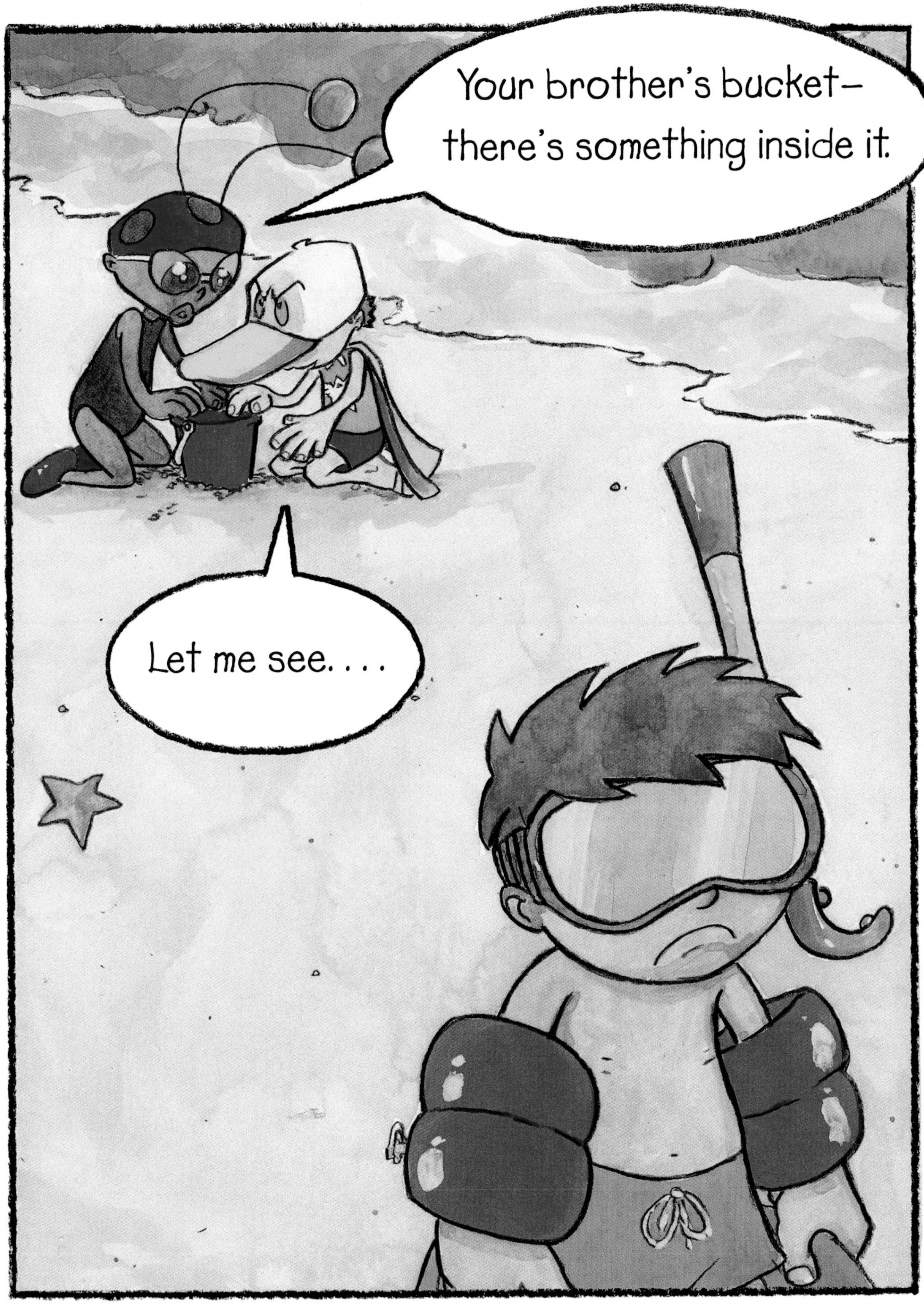
Your brother's bucket—
there's something inside it.
Let me see. . . .

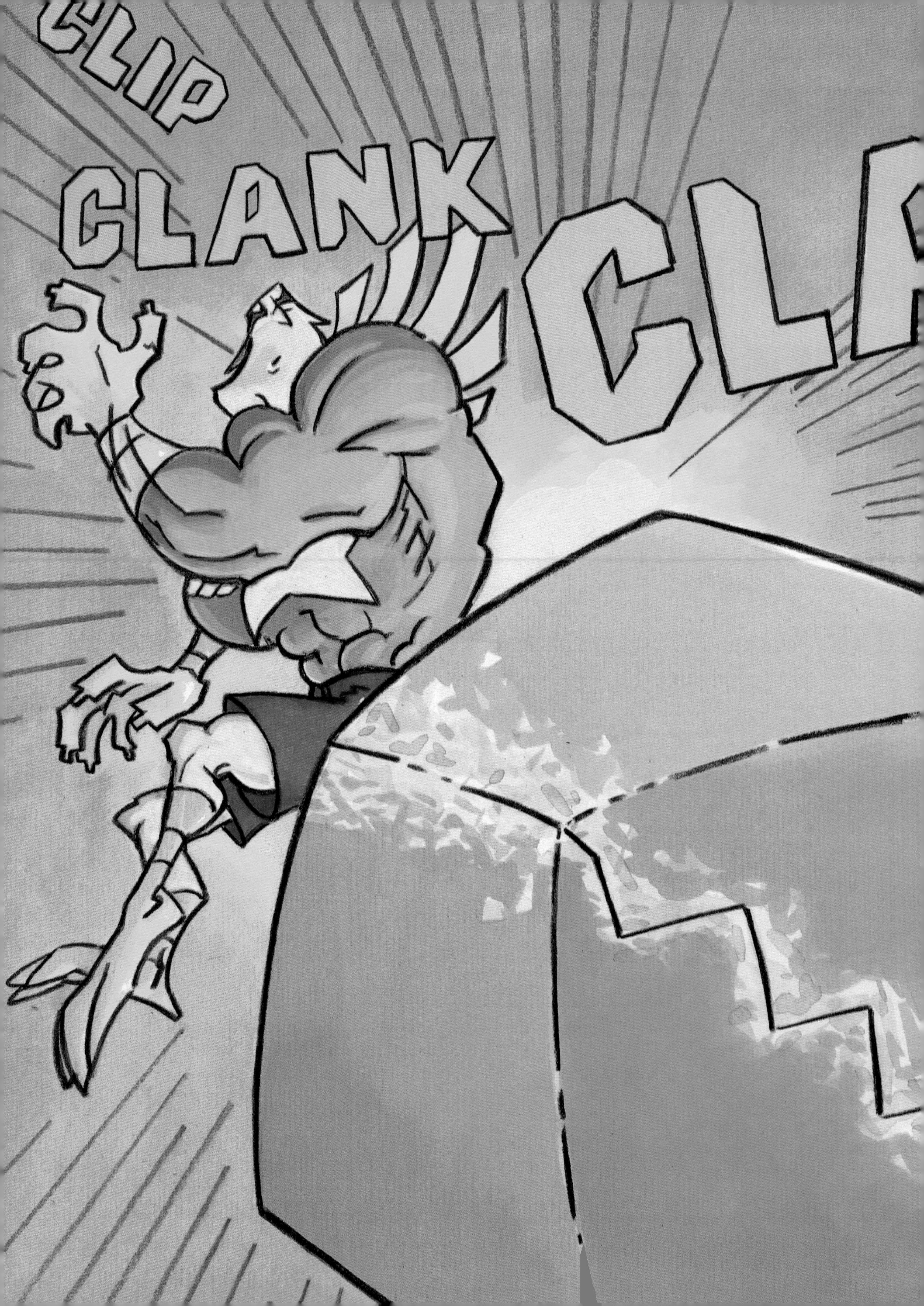
CLIP
CLANK

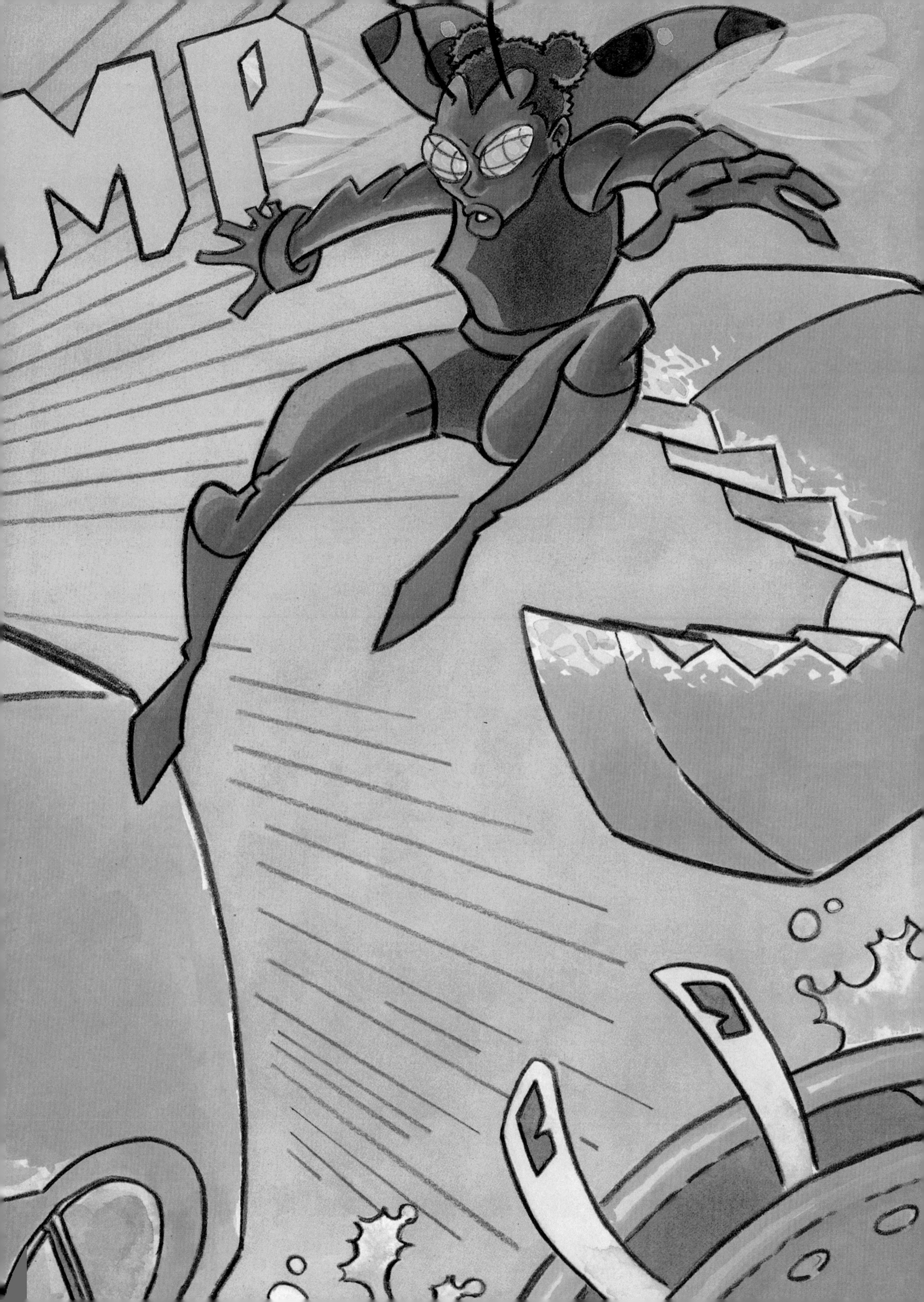
MP

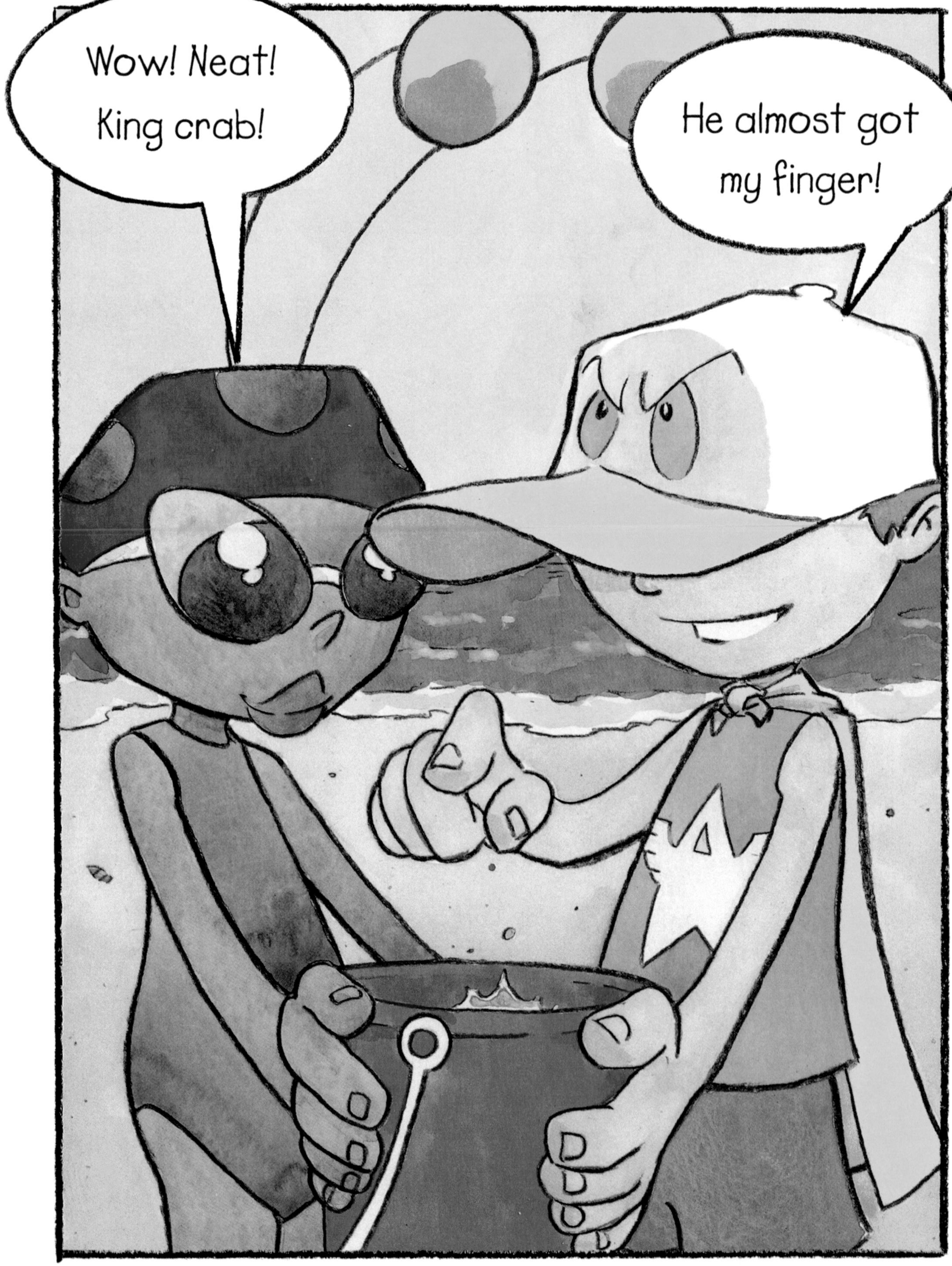
Wow! Neat! King crab!
He almost got my finger!

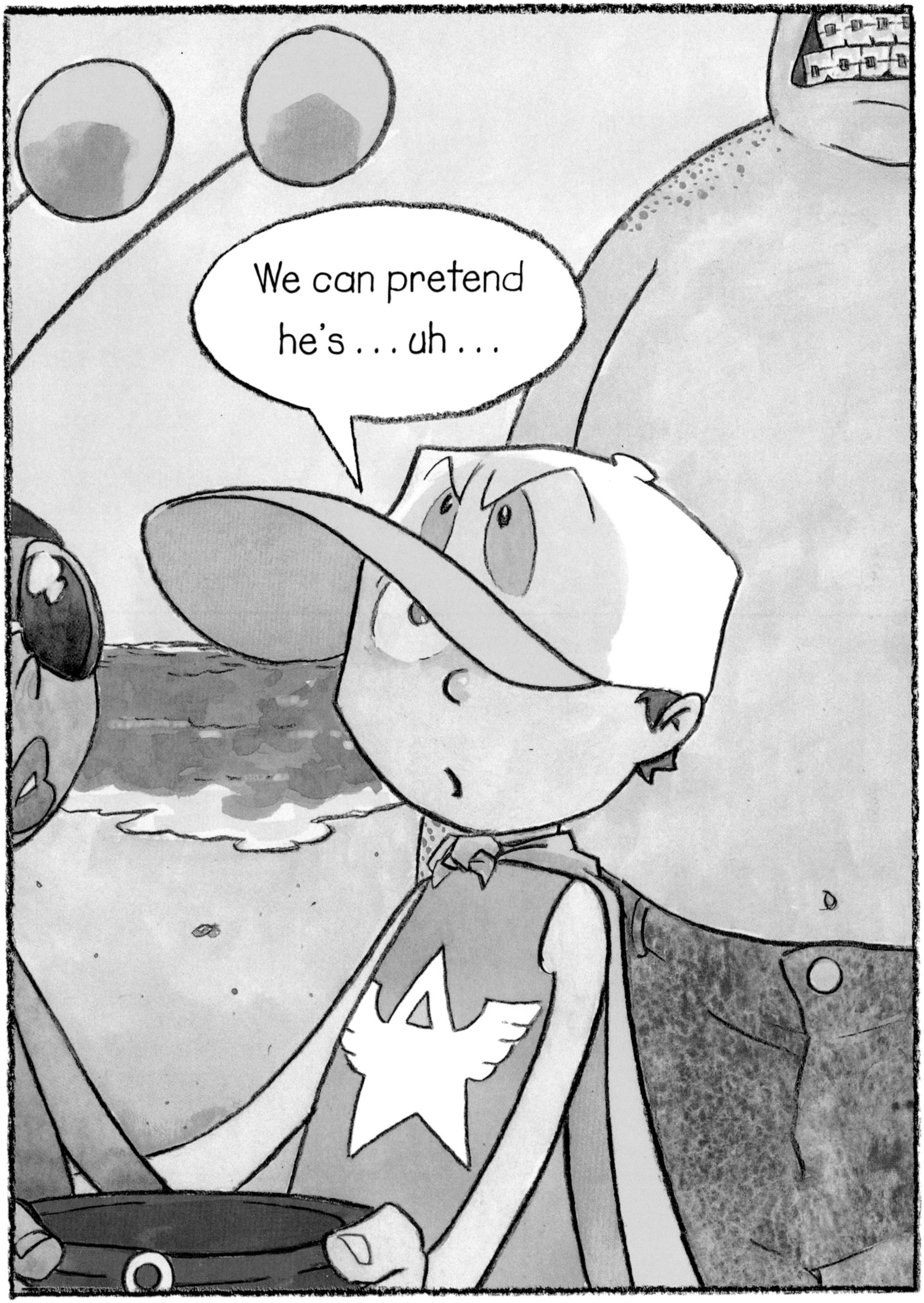
We can pretend he's . . . uh . . .

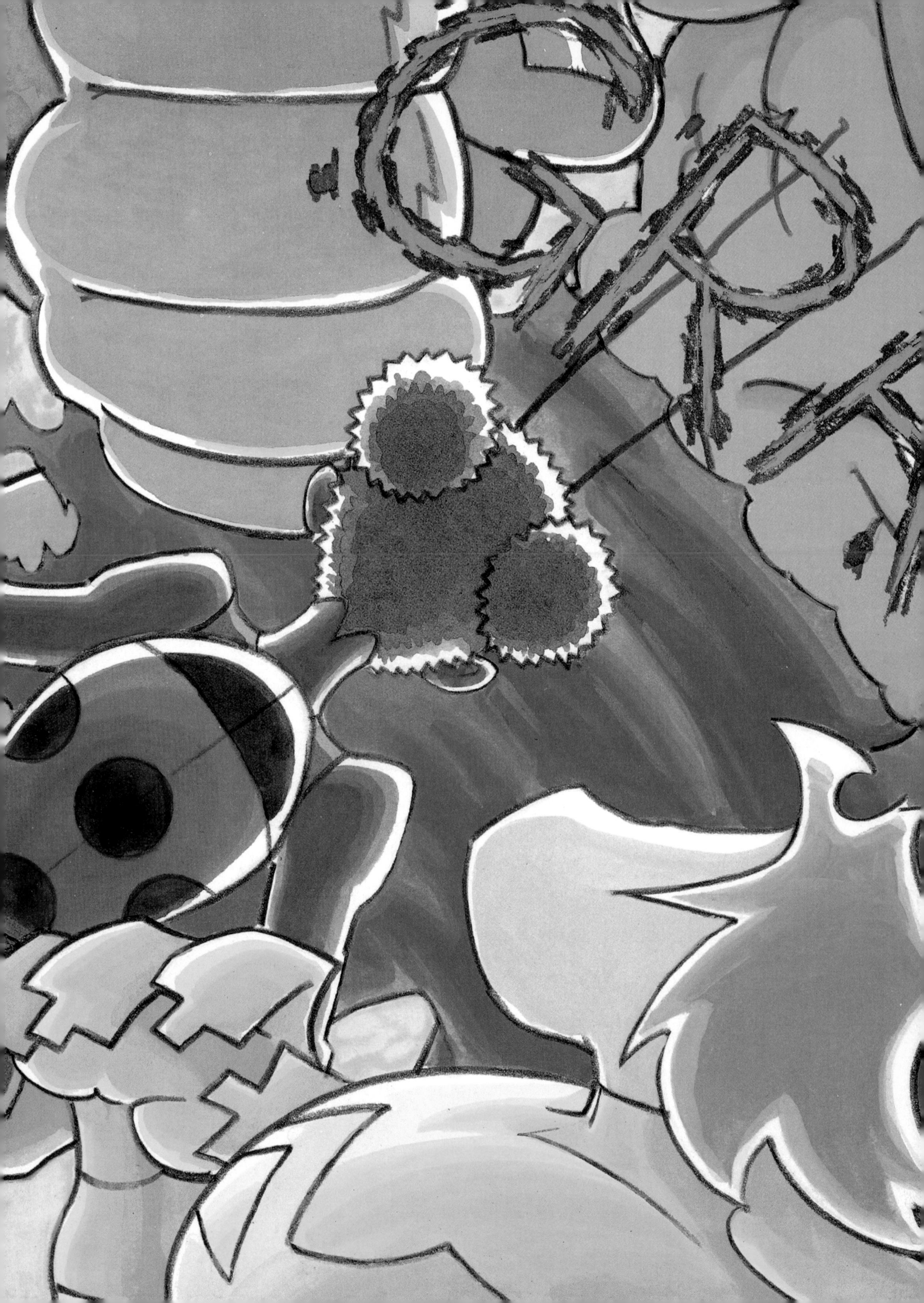

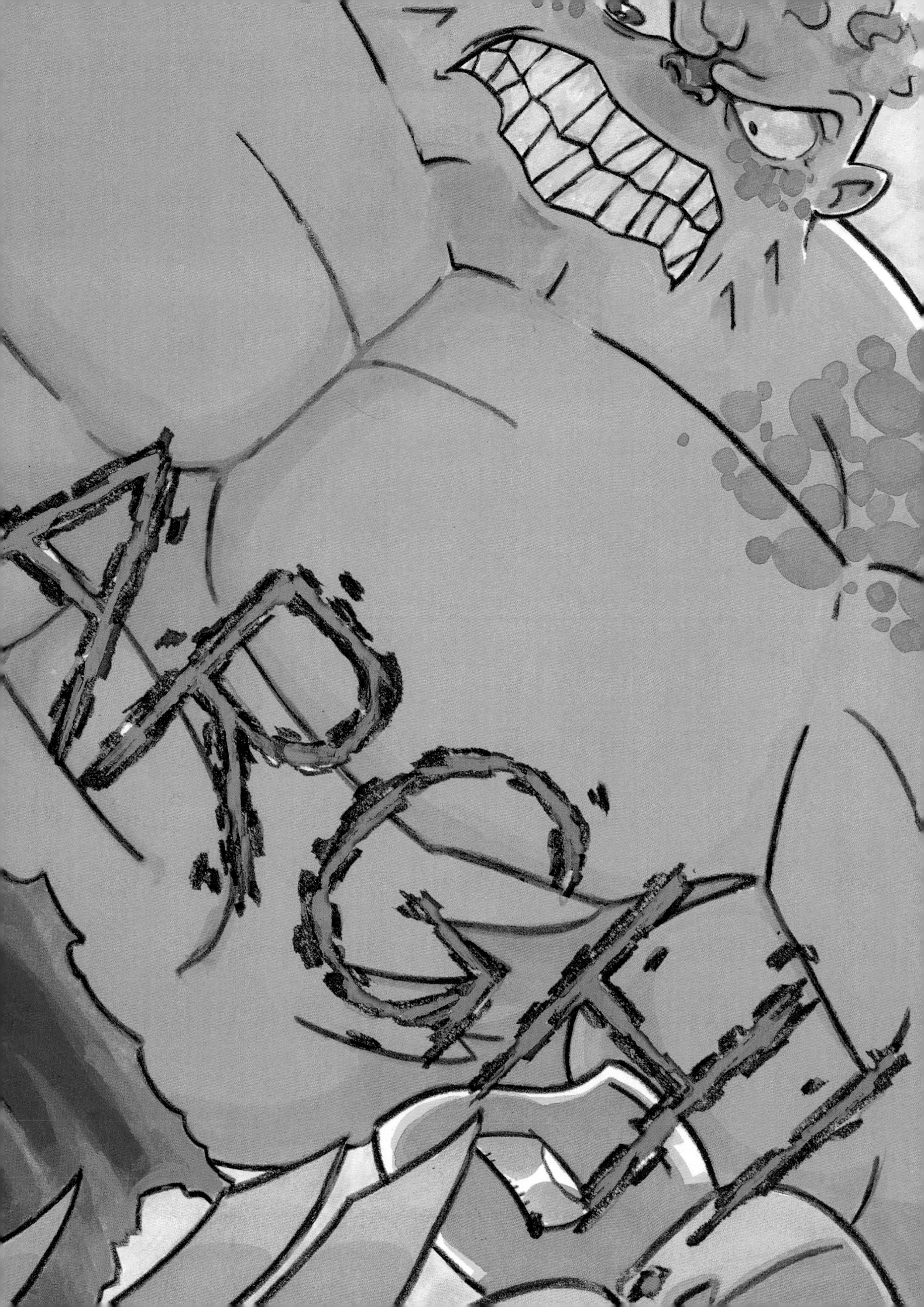
ARGH

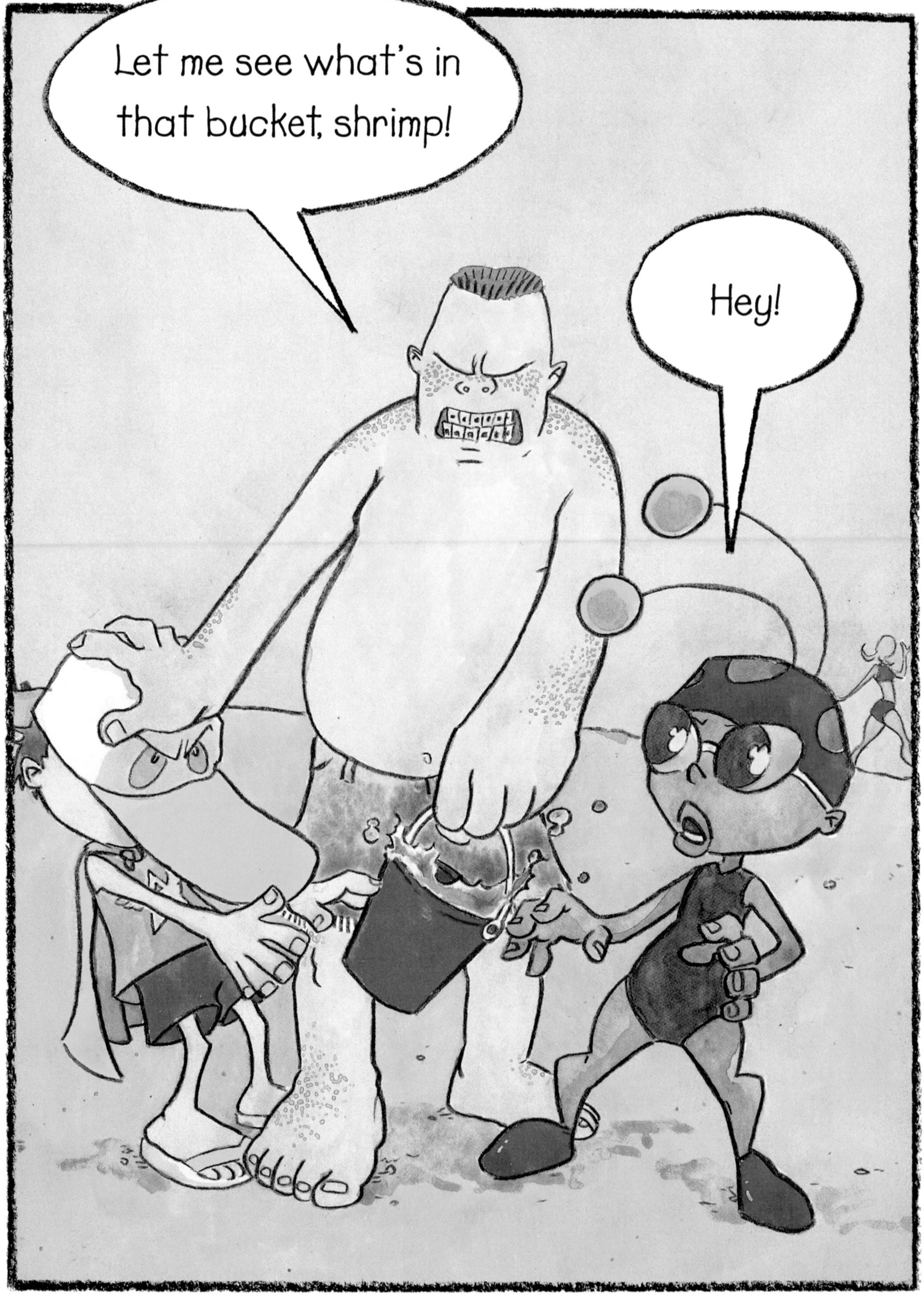
Let me see what's in that bucket, shrimp!
Hey!

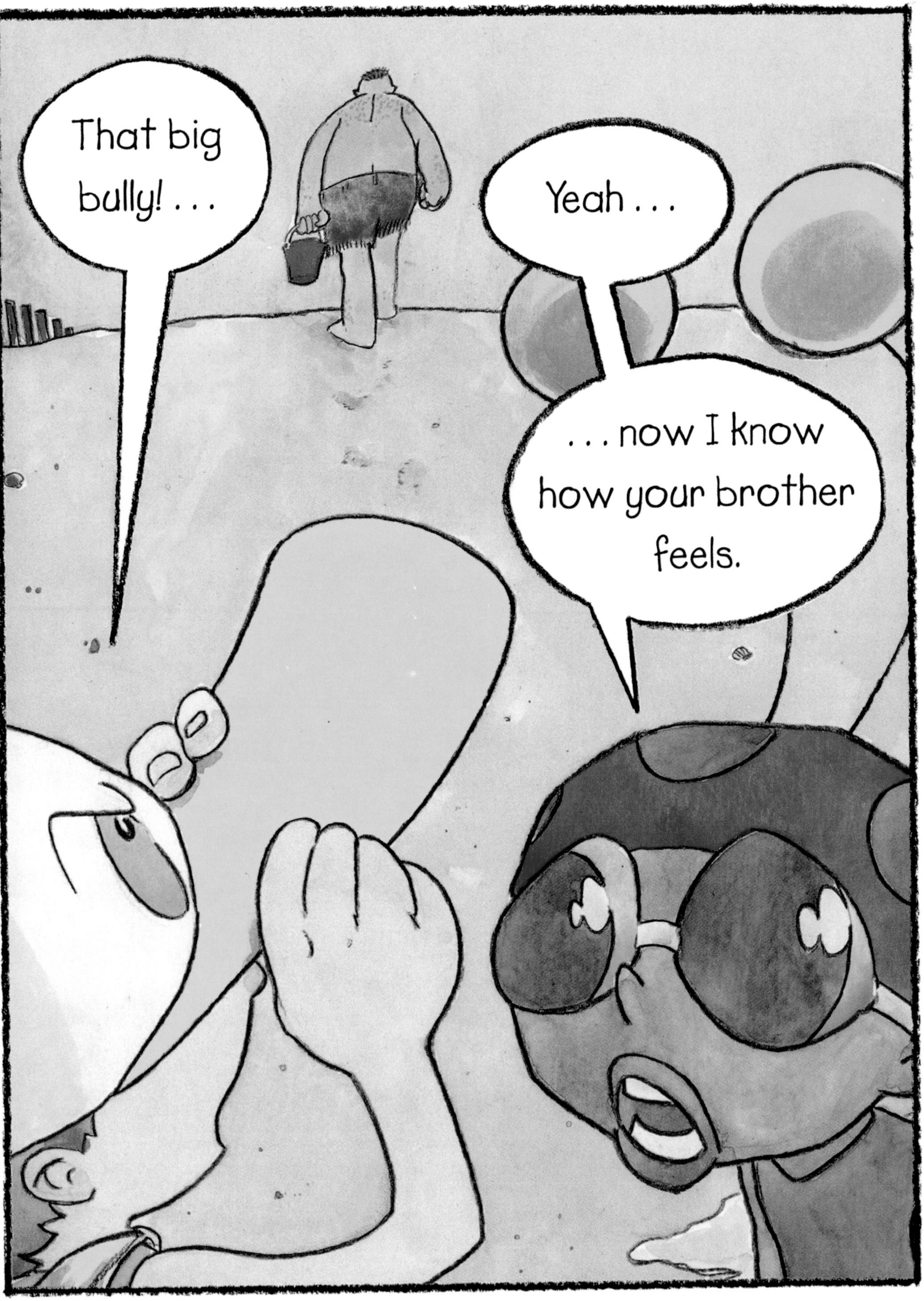
That big bully! . . .
Yeah . . .
. . . now I know how your brother feels.

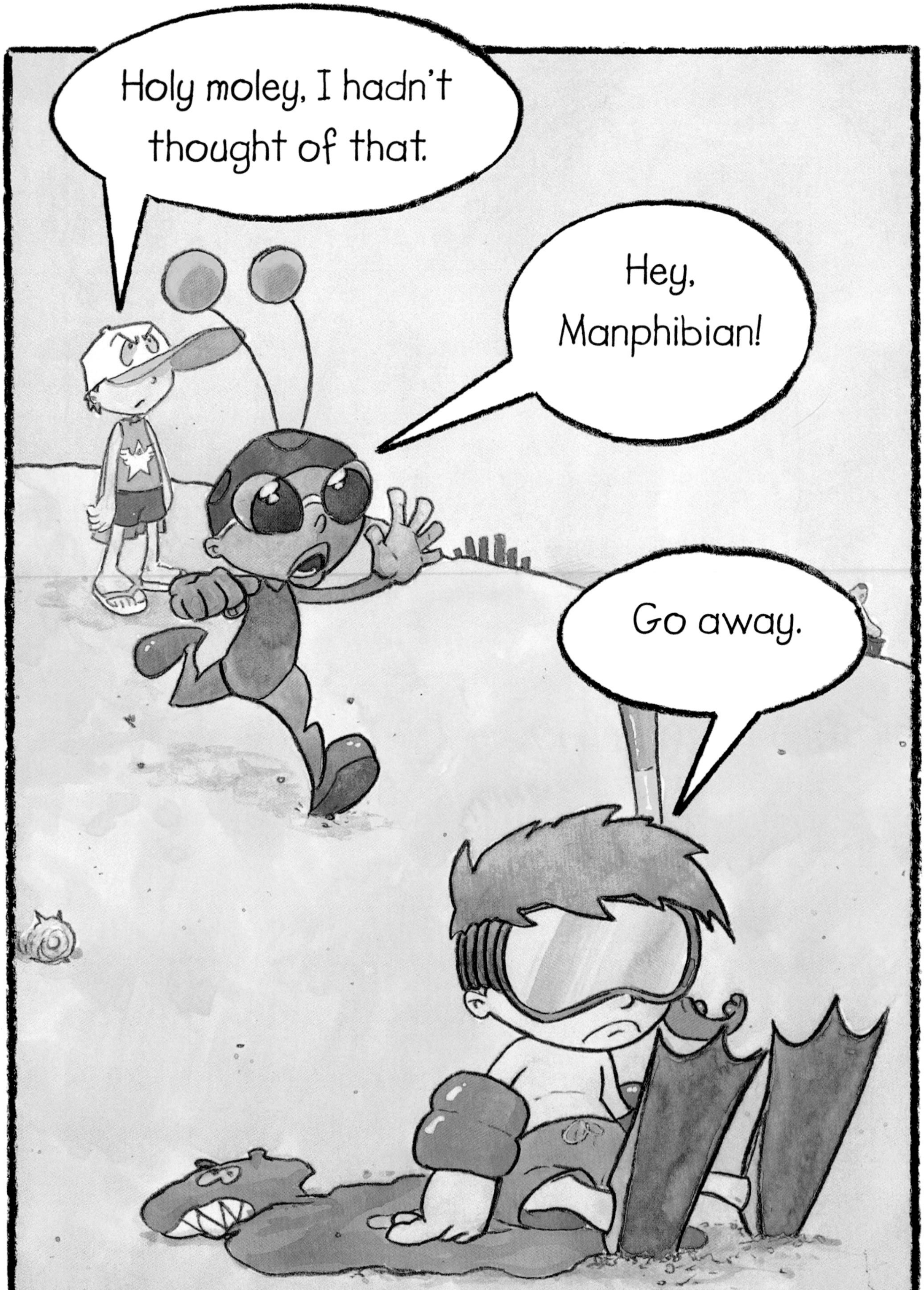
Holy moley, I hadn't thought of that.
Hey, Manphibian!
Go away.

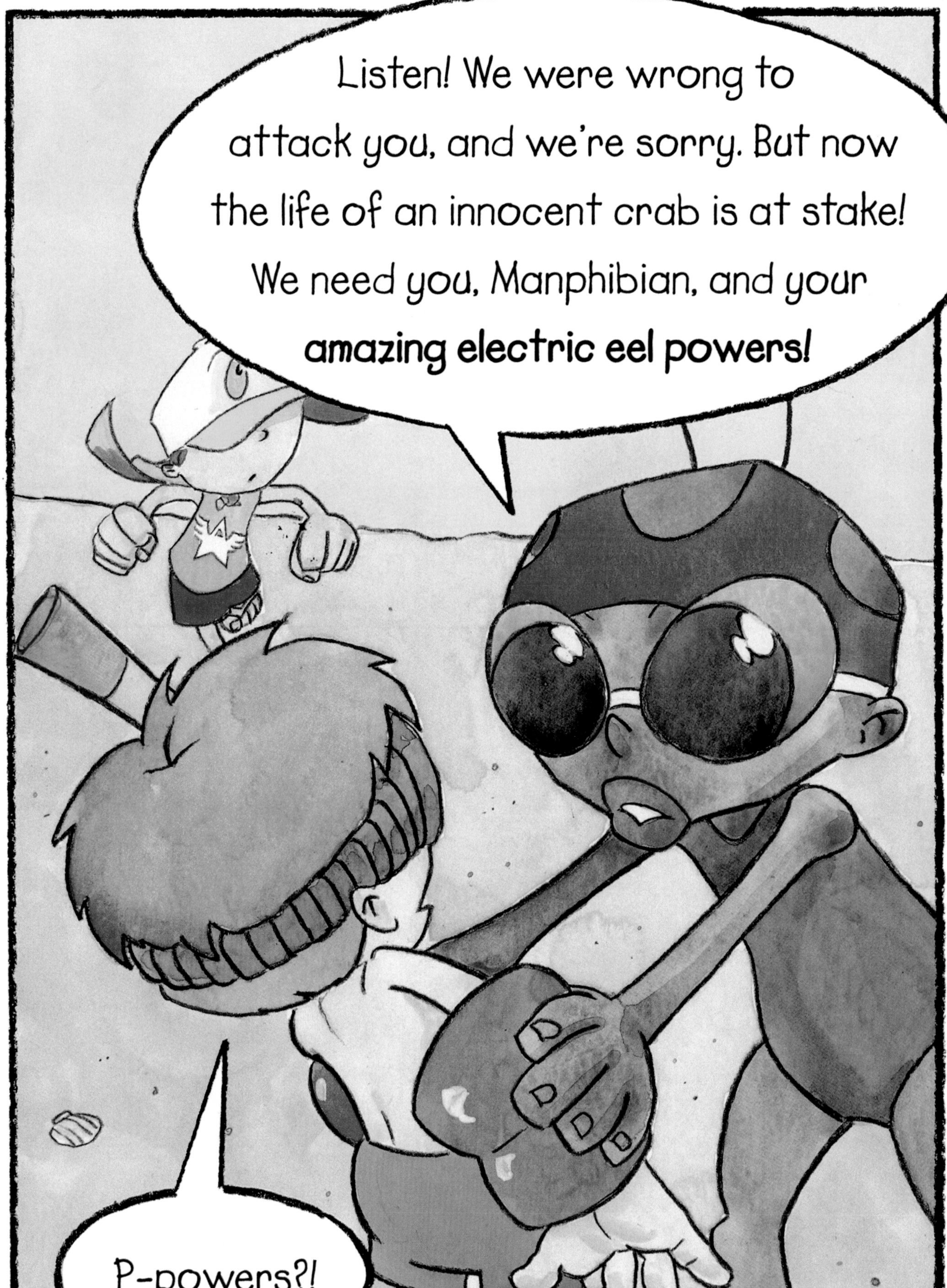
Listen! We were wrong to attack you, and we're sorry. But now the life of an innocent crab is at stake! We need you, Manphibian, and your **amazing electric eel powers!**
P-powers?!

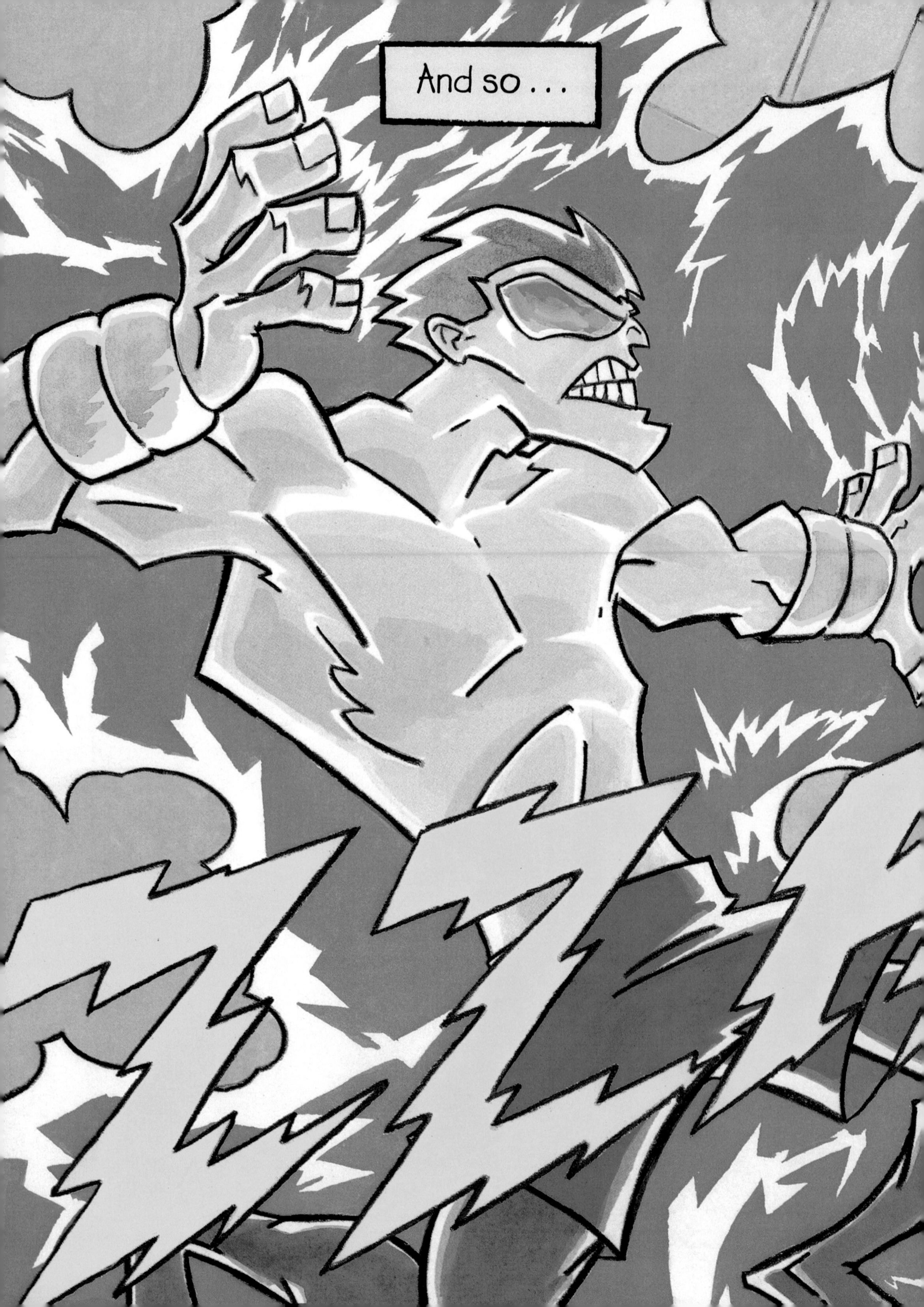
And so . . .

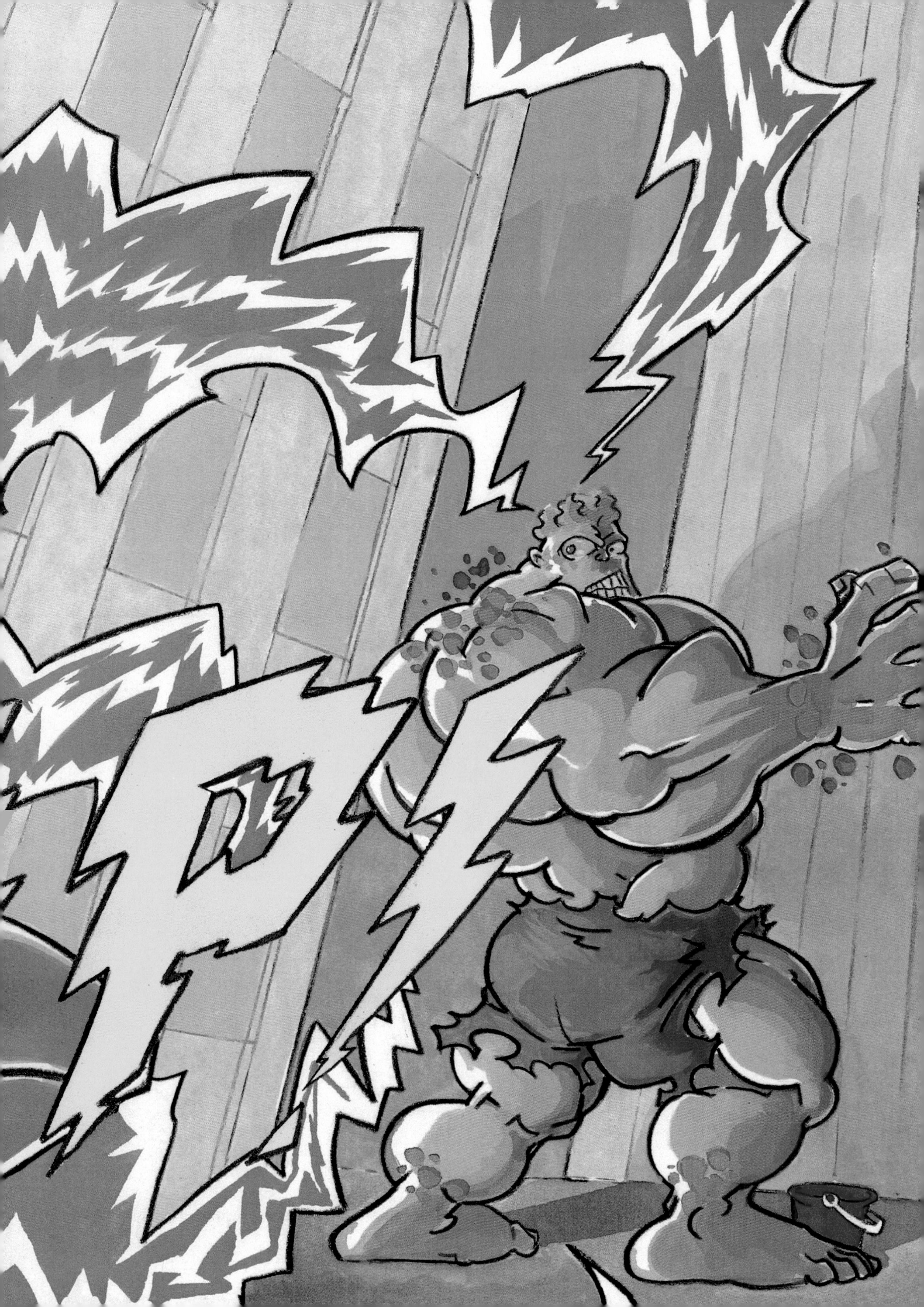

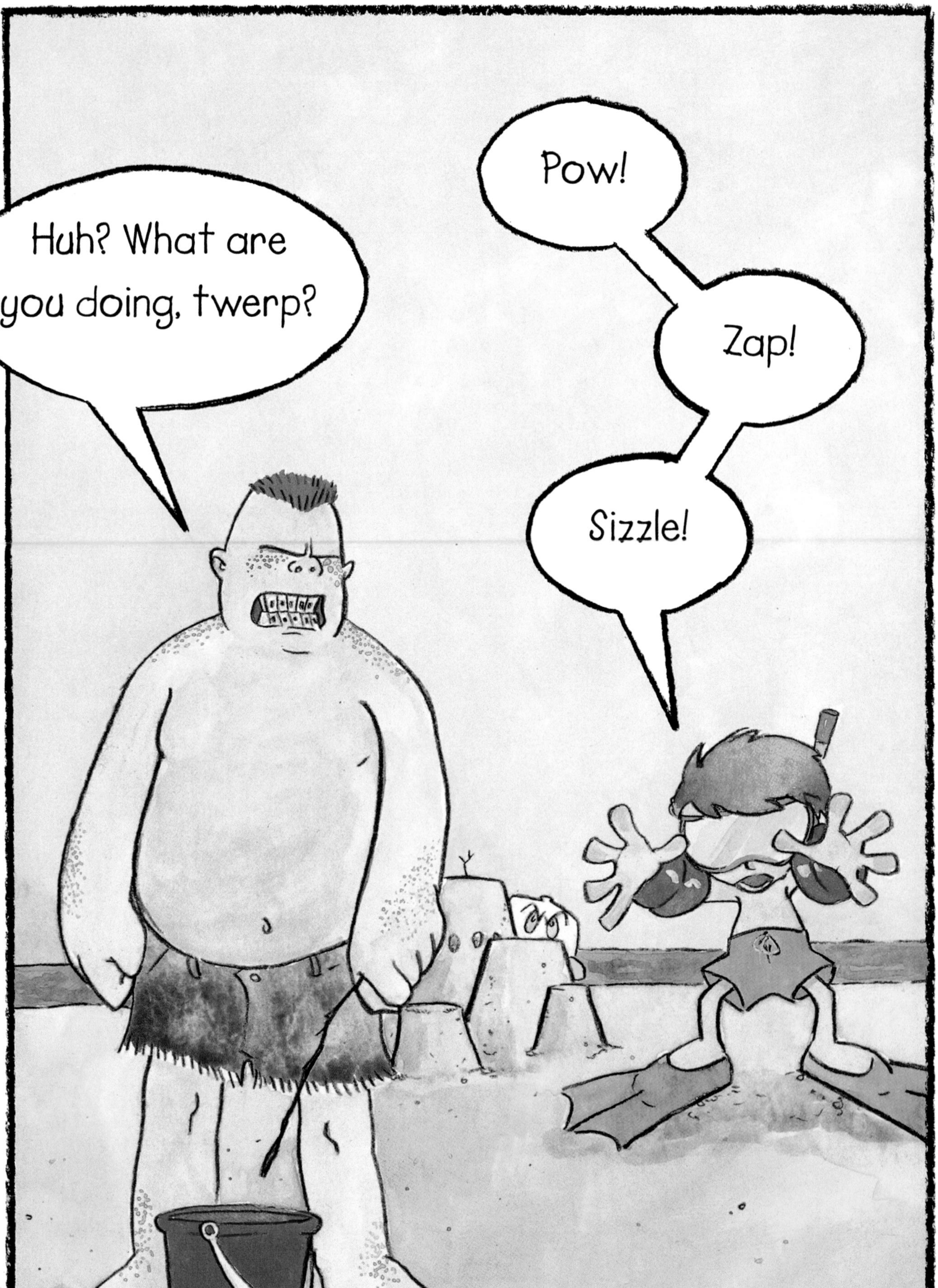
Huh? What are you doing, twerp?
Pow!
Zap!
Sizzle!

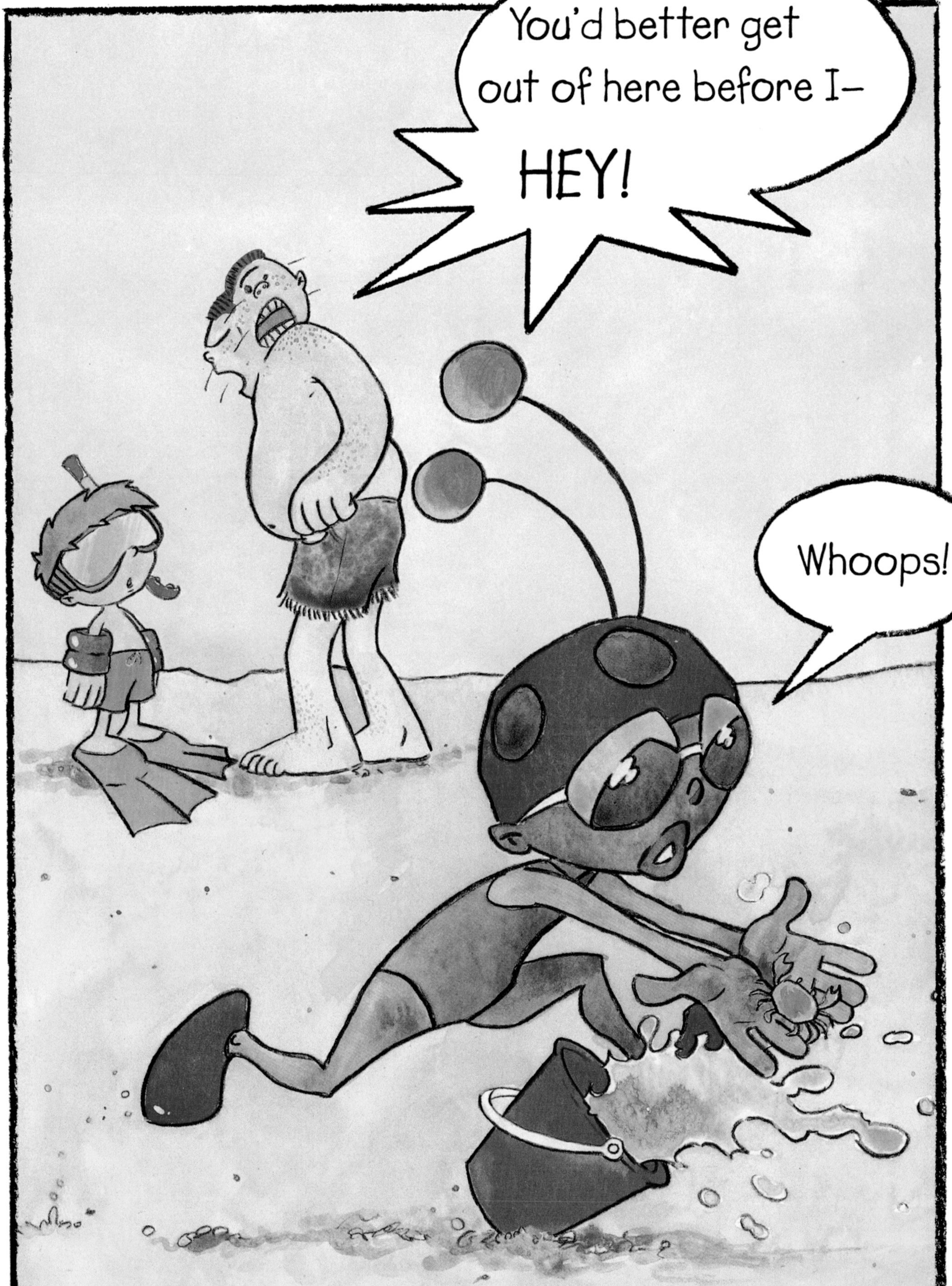
You'd better get out of here before I–
HEY!
Whoops!

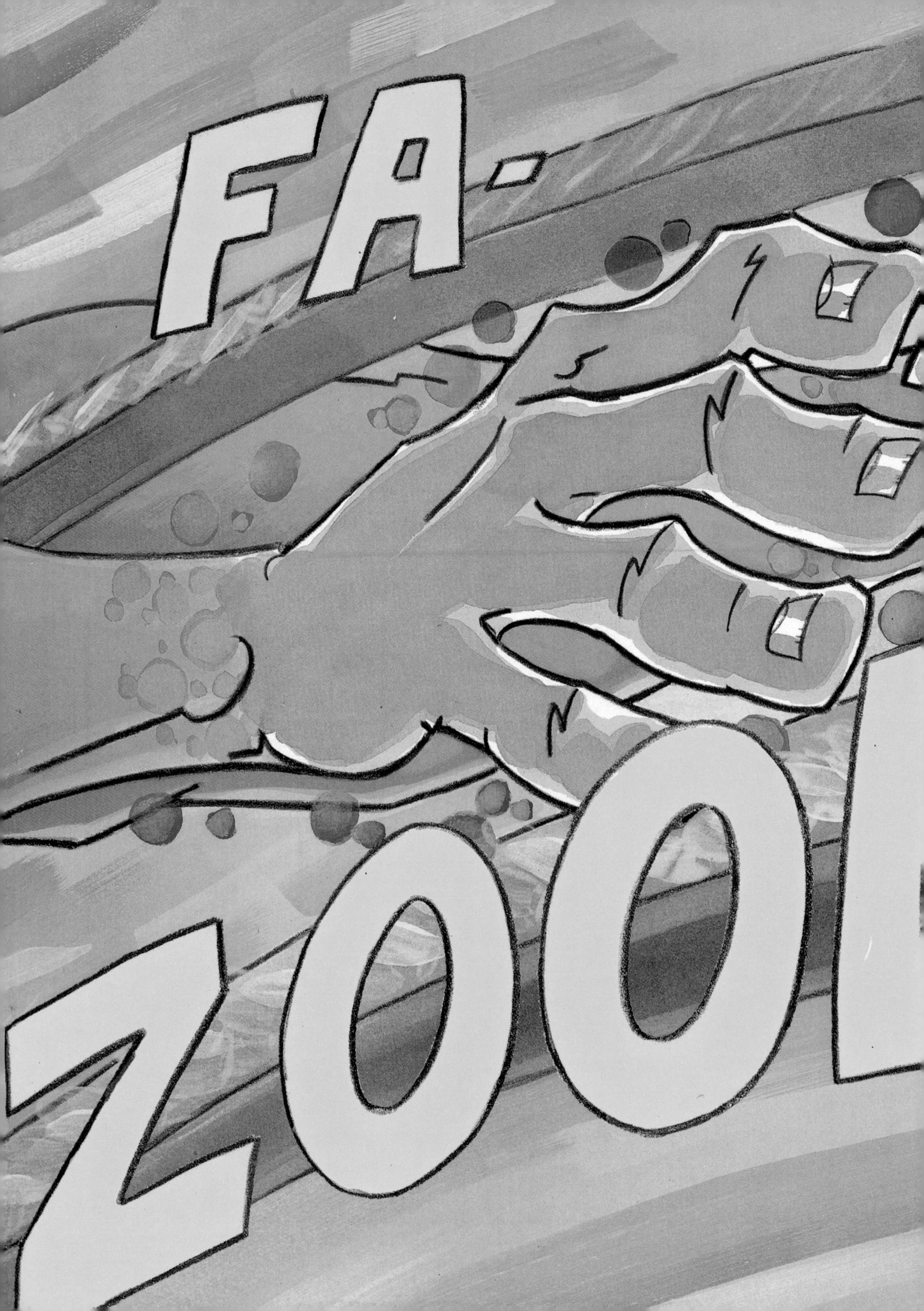
FA-
ZOO

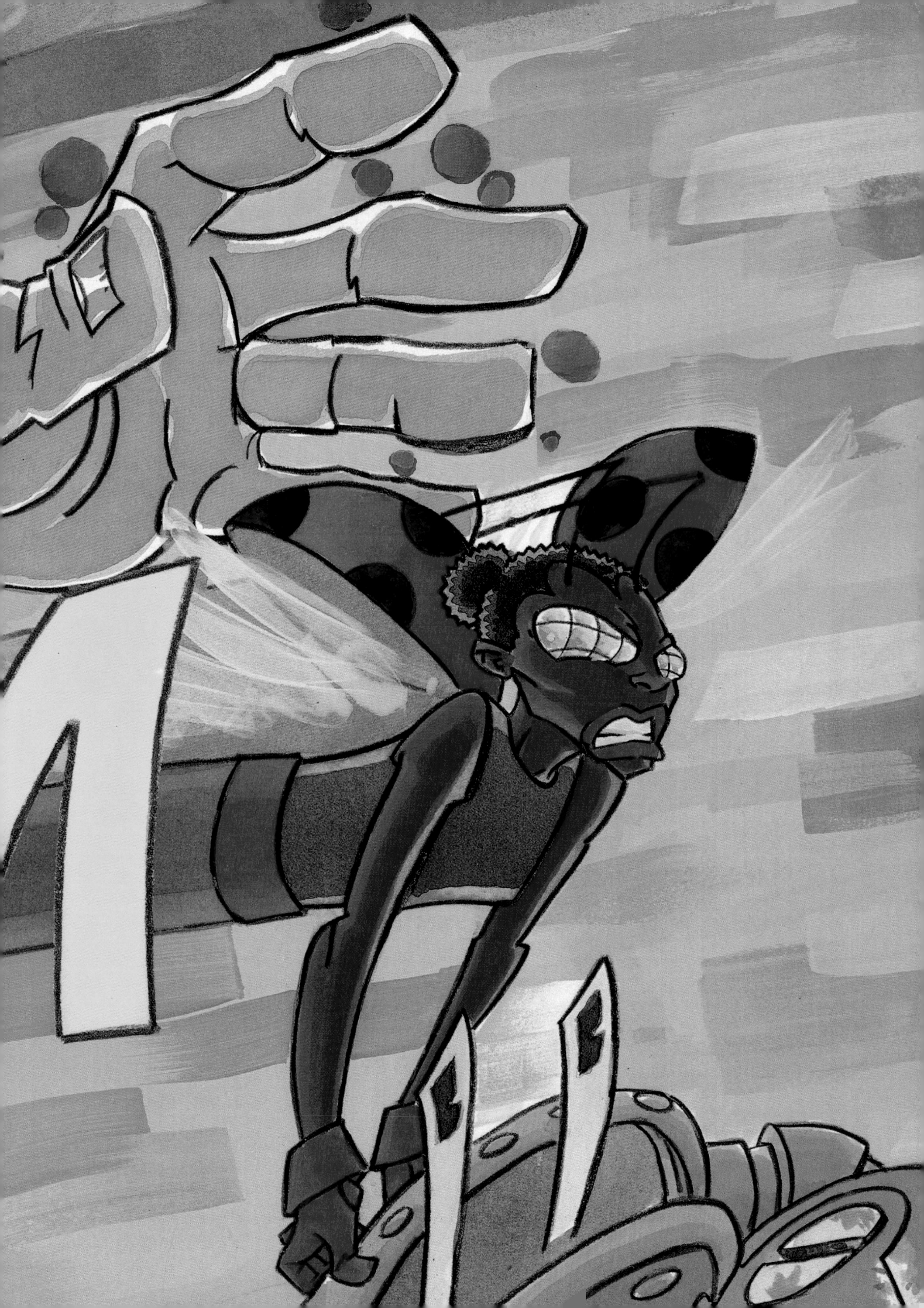

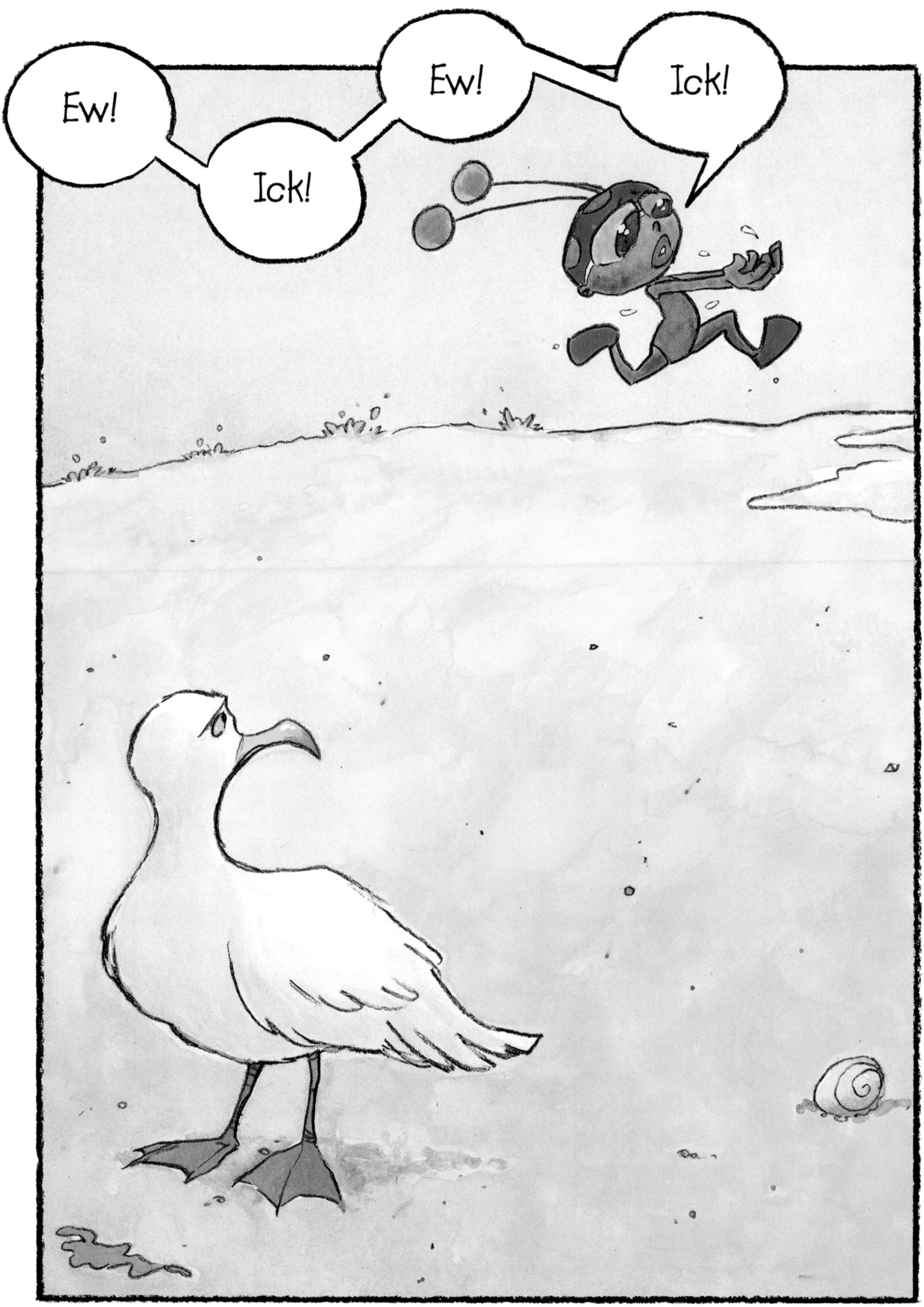
Ew!
Ick!
Ew!
Ick!

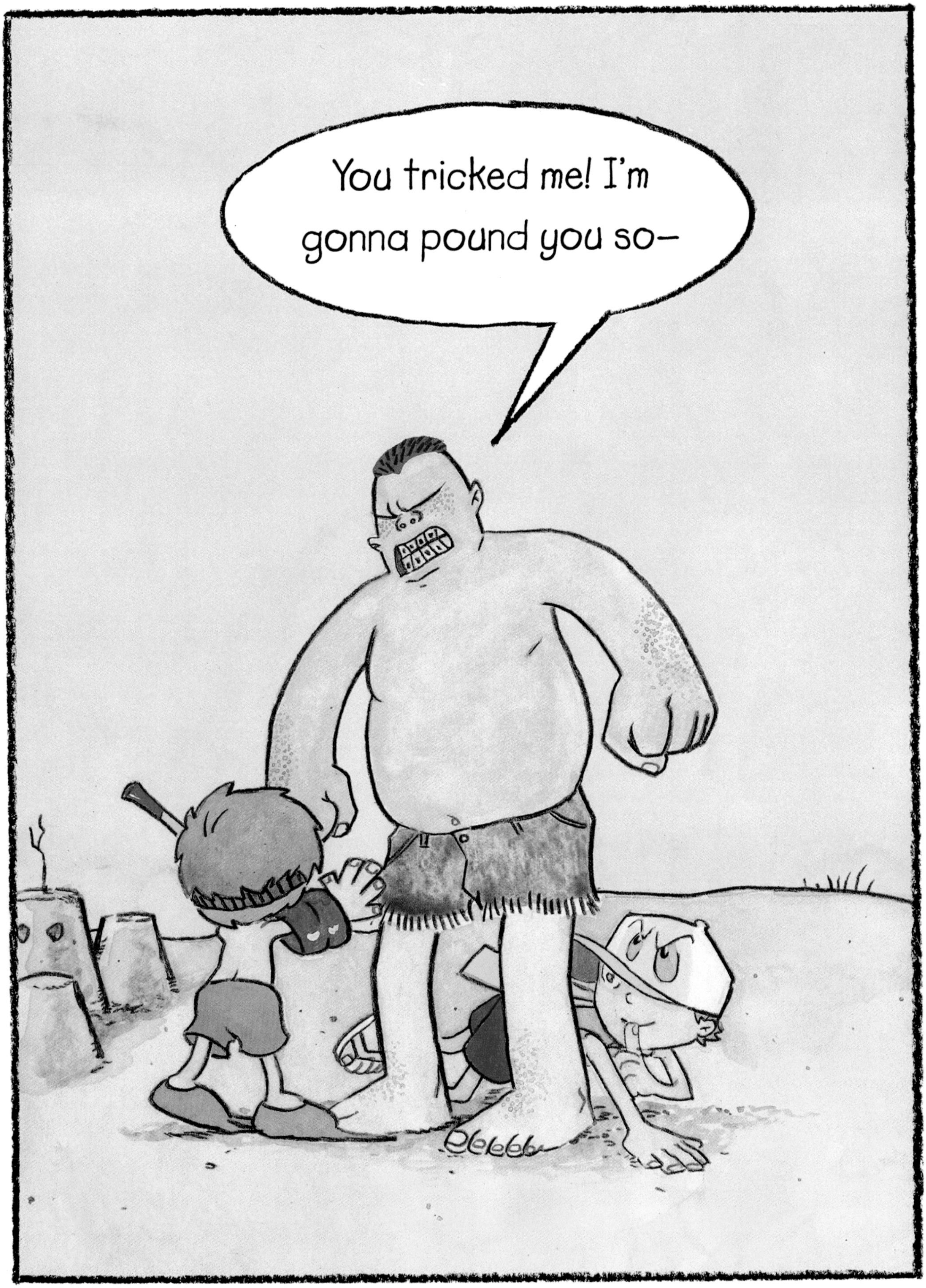
You tricked me! I'm gonna pound you so–

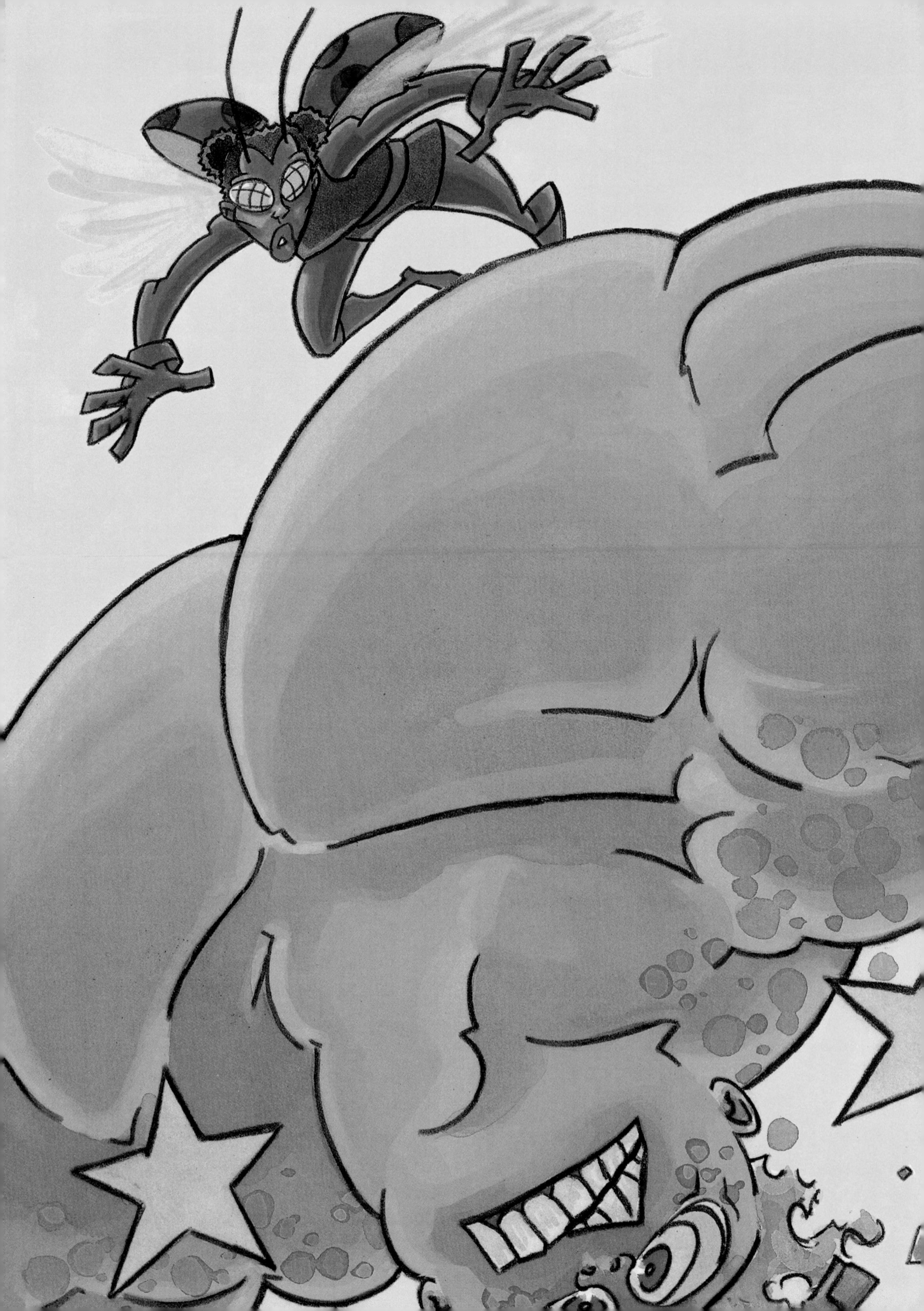

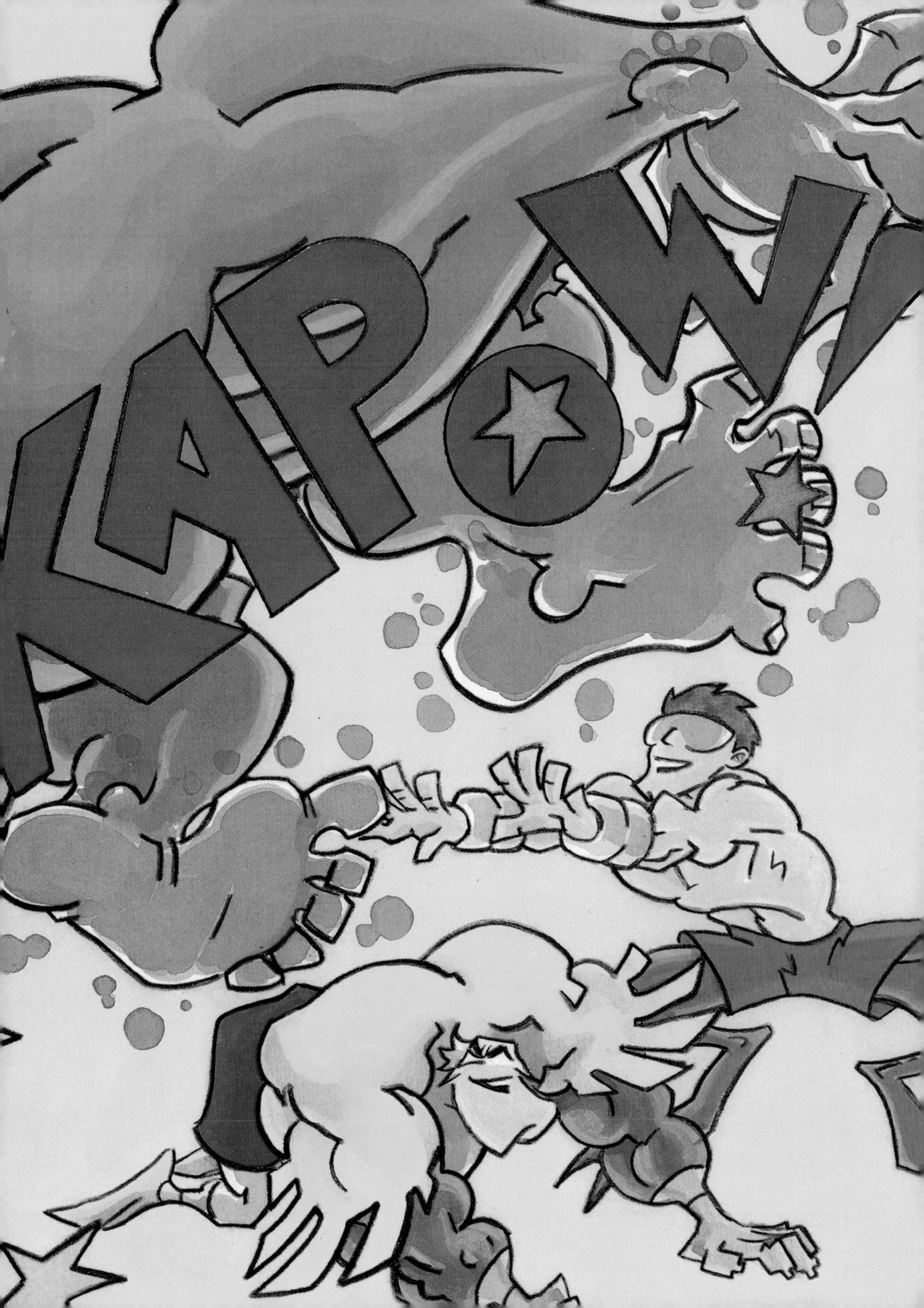
KAPOW!

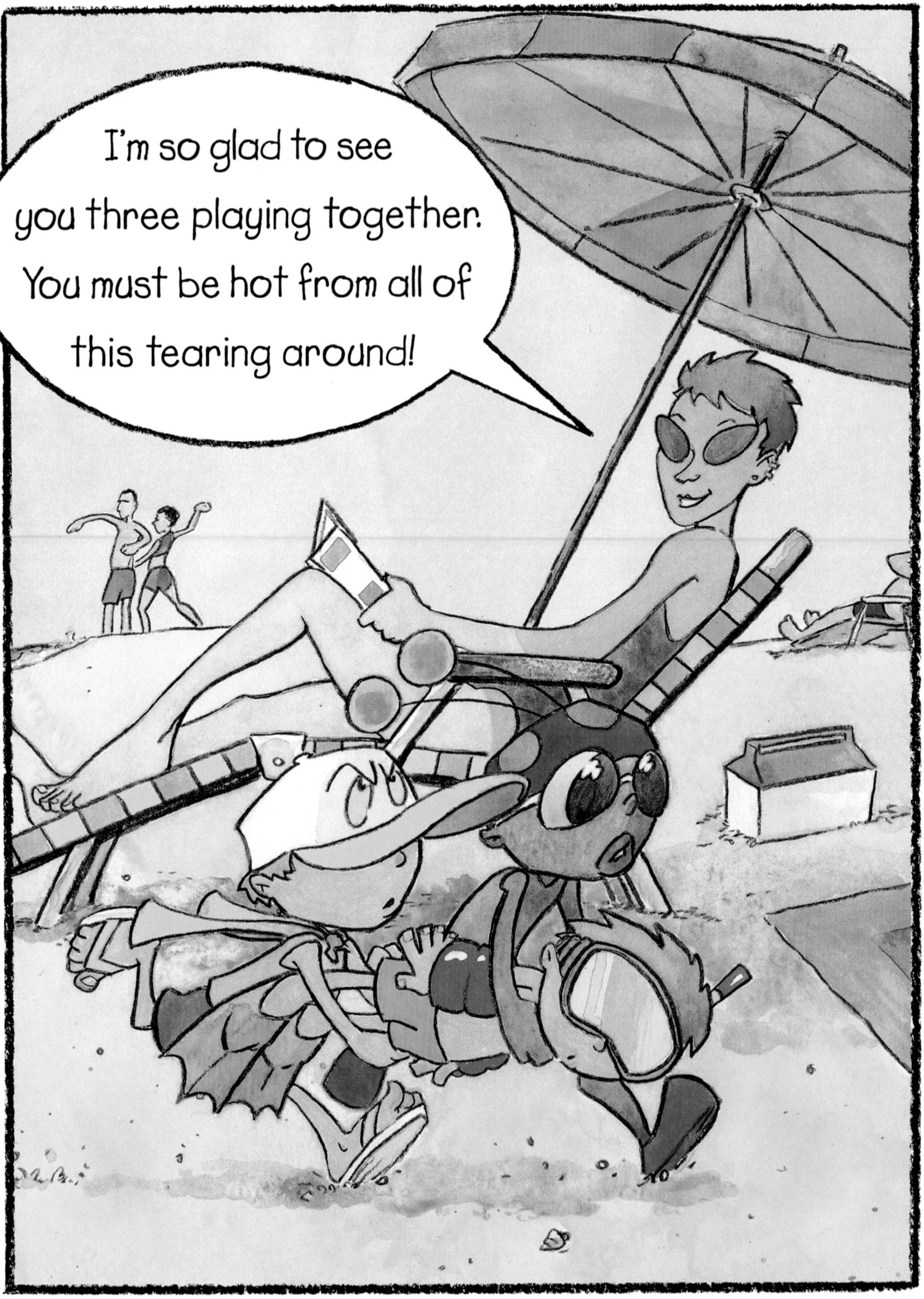
I'm so glad to see you three playing together. You must be hot from all of this tearing around!

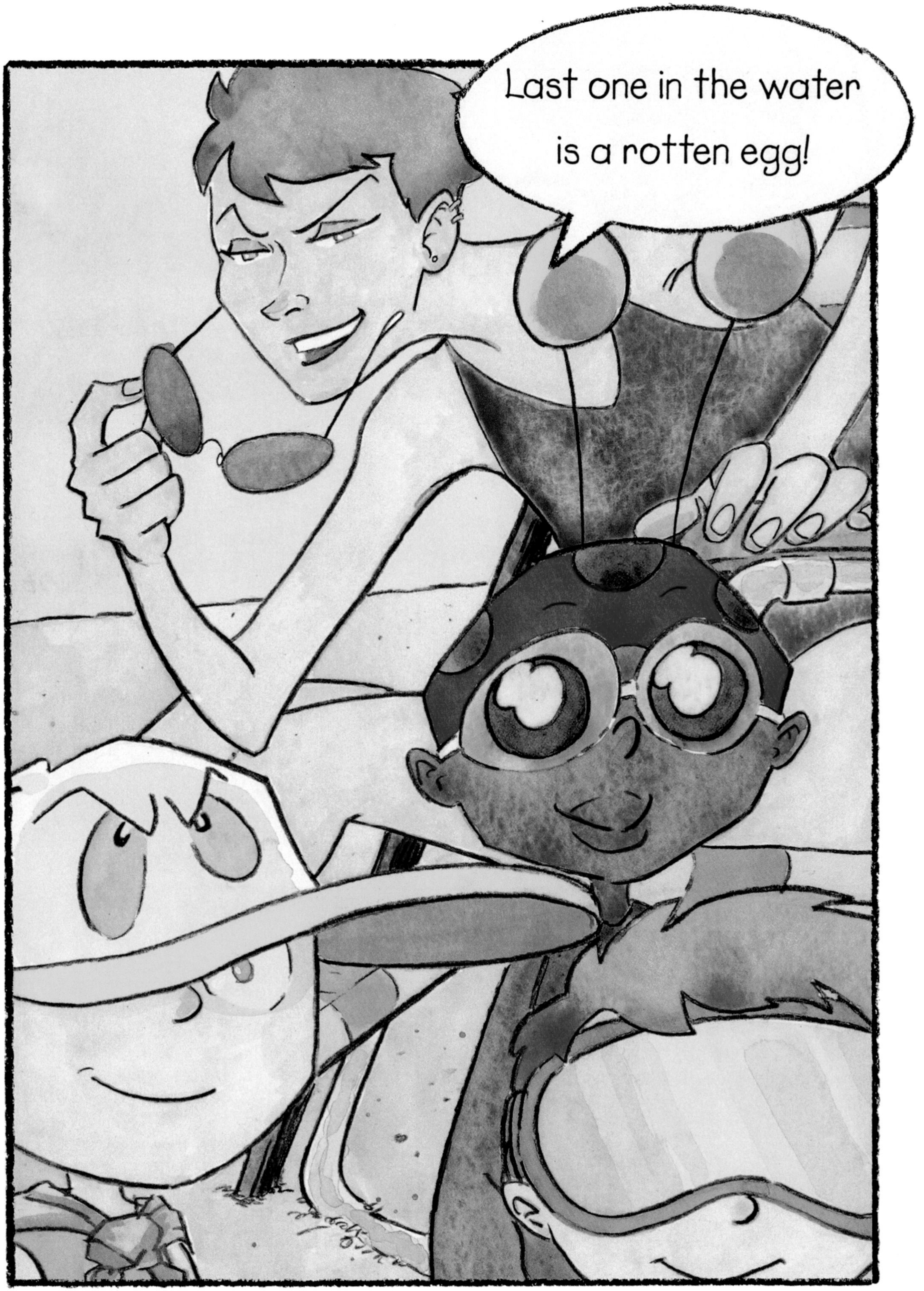
Last one in the water is a rotten egg!

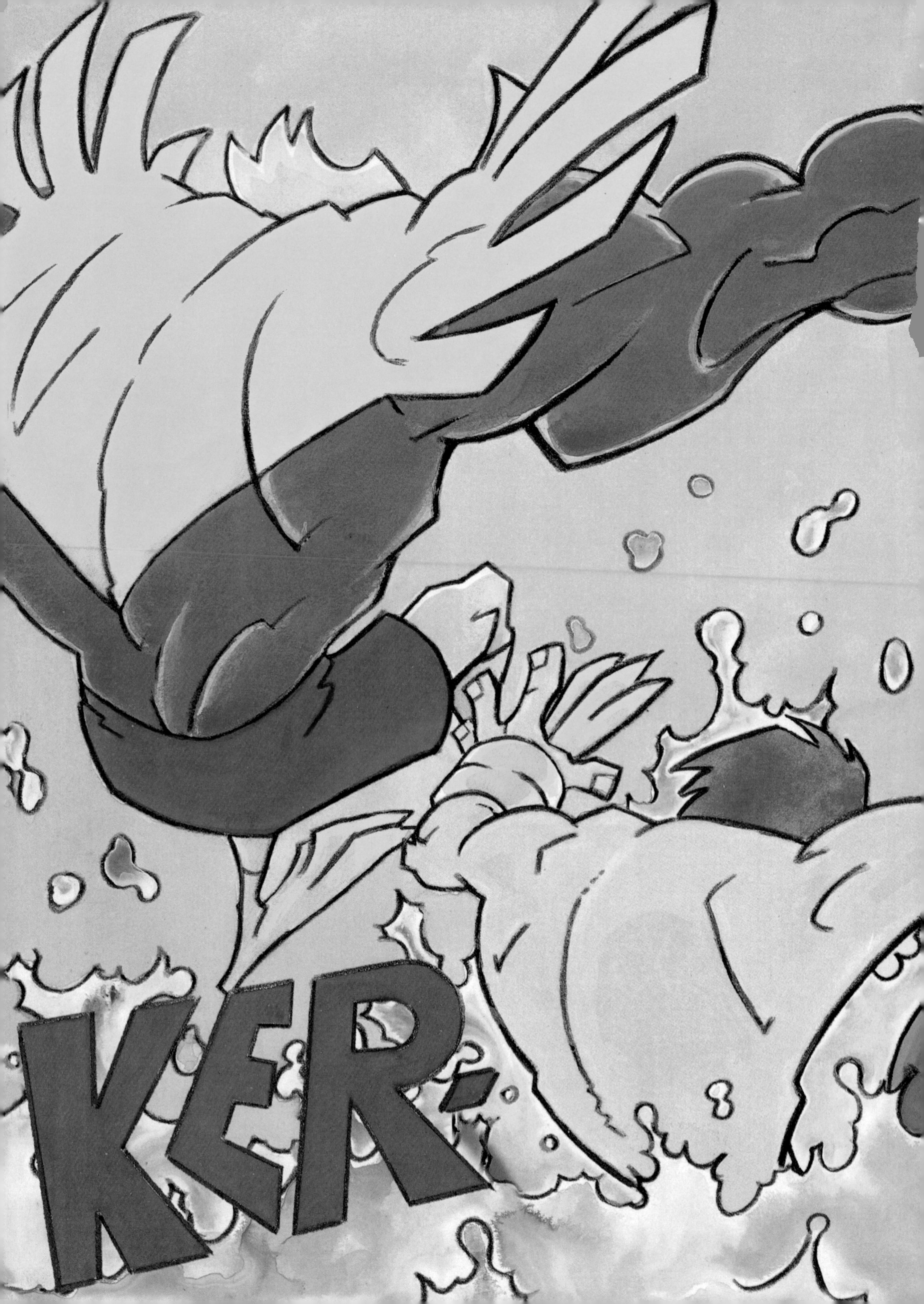
KER-

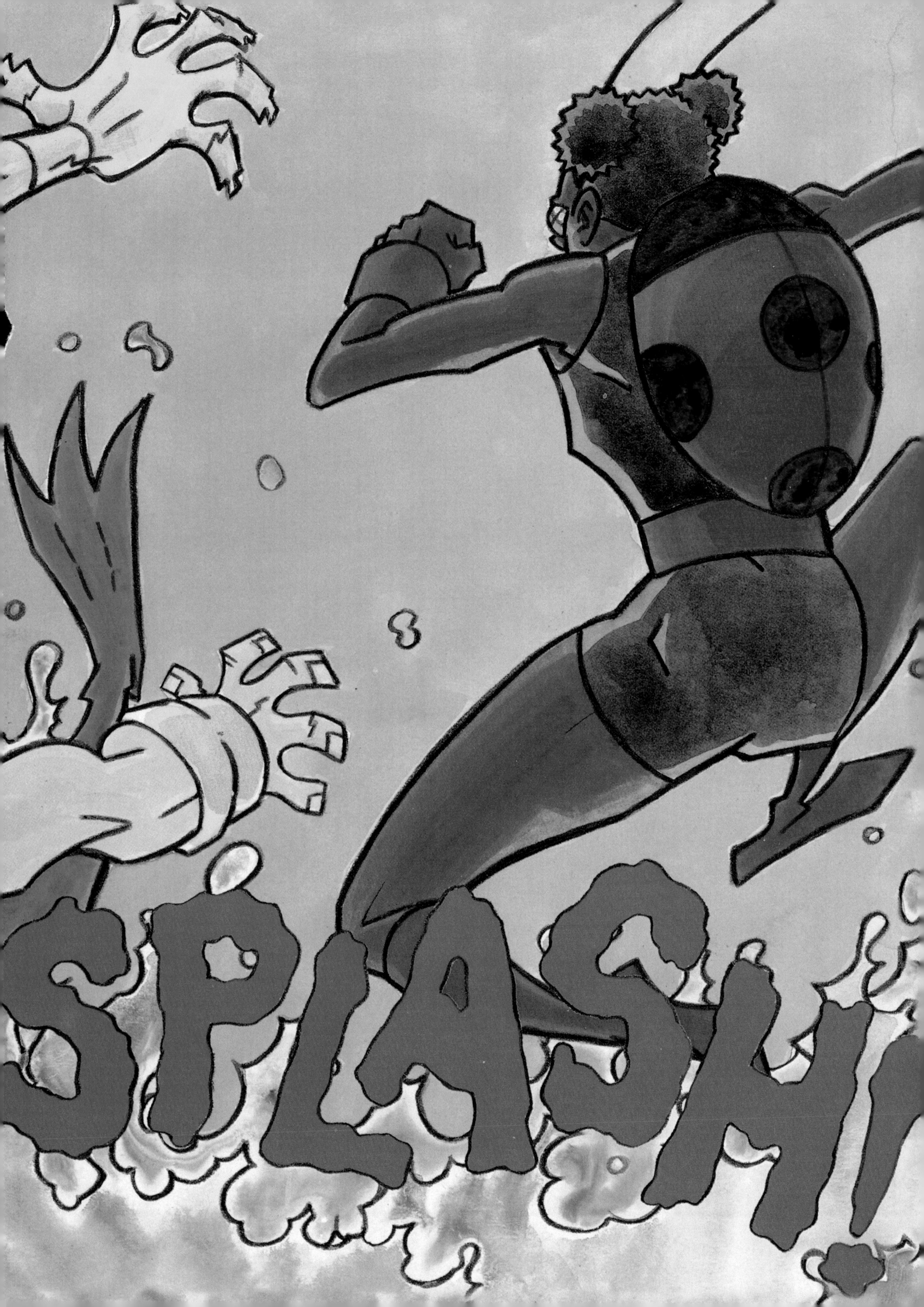
SPLASH!

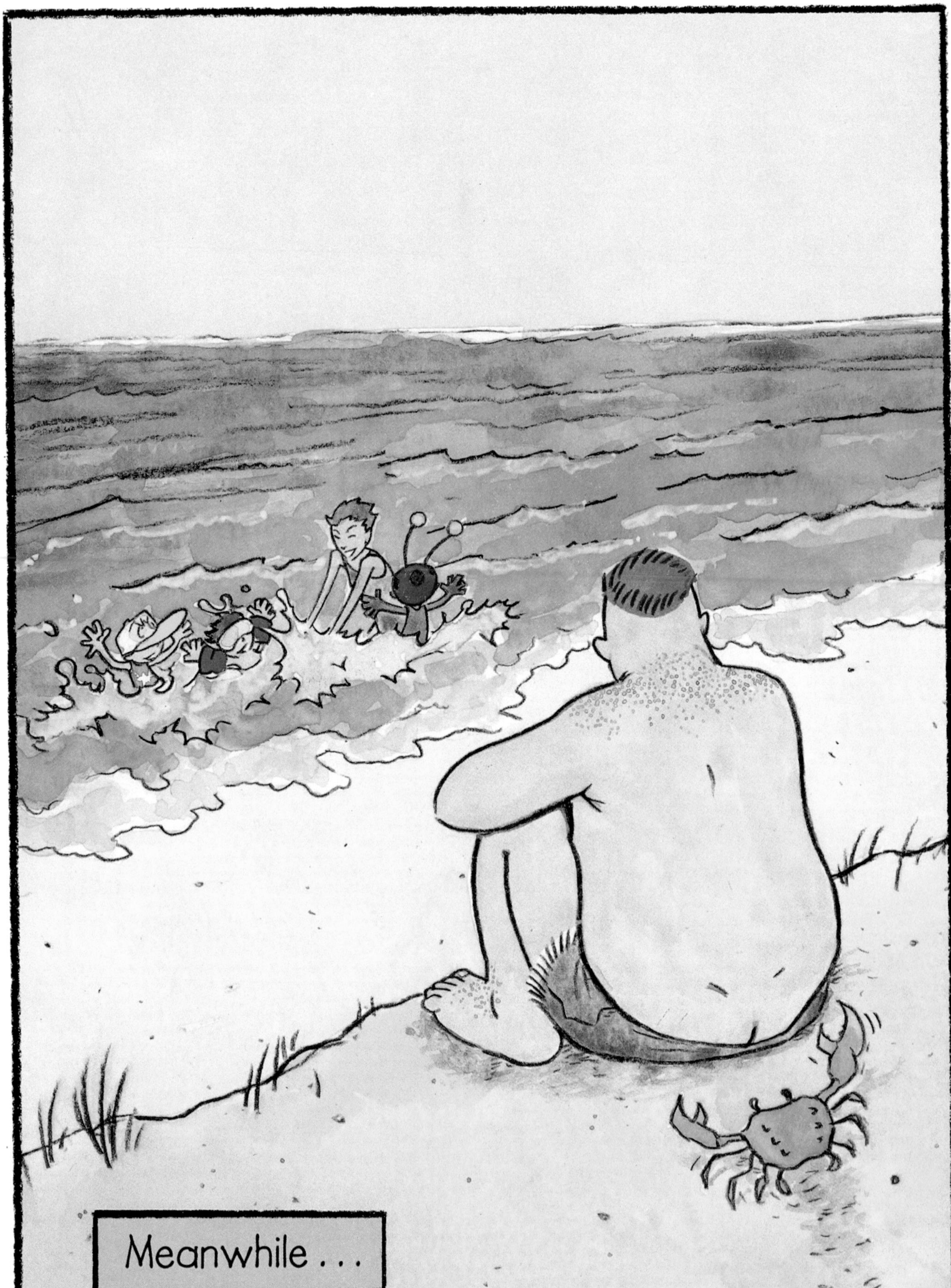
Meanwhile . . .